DEATH
DO US PART

Short stories: Proceed at your own risk

J.L. Salter
Charles A. Salter

To Dr. Brian Reamy, with gratitude and respect.

Charles A. Salter

δ
Dingbat Publishing
Humble, Texas

DEATH DO US PART
Copyright © 2019 by J.L. Salter and Charles A. Salter
Primary Print ISBN 978-1-654260736

Published by Dingbat Publishing
Humble, Texas

Table of Contents

Dedications

J. L. Salter

To Mrs. Theresa Fleming—my teacher for eighth grade English and homeroom—who, in many ways, was the first person (outside of family) to encourage my writing.

Charles A. Salter

To my wife Carlota, the love of my life.

Buddies Forever

J. L. Salter

March 9, 1971
WHEN I CAME TO, I was blind. I could feel I was on a bed... but it was a lot more comfortable than my regular bunk at Fire Base *Mary Ann*, an Army position south of Da Nang and way too close to the DMZ. "Where am I and why can't I see anything?" When my fingers began scratching at my face, I felt cloth and tape.

"Relax, soldier," said a kind male voice, obviously trying to reassure me. "You're in the 95th Evacuation Hospital now and your eyes are bandaged."

Wondered how I got that far north to Da Nang. Last thing I recalled was the explosion outside my fire base perimeter. "Doc, am I blind?"

"I'm Chaplain Harris, son. You'll need to get your status from the medical staff, but it's my understanding your eyeballs caught a few slivers of metal or something."

They felt as though they were filled with needles. "So I'll be able to see after these bandages are off?"

The chaplain's warm fleshy hand covered mine. "The impression I got was that you'll be just fine, but your eyes have to heal before they can test your vision."

"Where's my buddy, Donahue?"

"I thought you were Donahue," he replied. And he made some noise at the foot of my bed—maybe the padre had my chart.

"No, I'm Donague... pronounced Don-ah-GHEE. Me and Donahue are buddies and they're always getting my name mixed up with his." After a second to let that sink in, I continued. "Is Donahue okay?"

The clipboard papers rustled some more. "Not sure, soldier. Was your buddy also injured in that blast?"

"I don't know, Chaplain. I just woke up and don't even know how I got here or how long I've been out of it. Much less anything about my buddy Donahue. That's why I'm asking you."

He obviously had no idea. "I understand the VC blew up your bunker pretty bad."

"It wasn't VC. It was one of our own grenades." The 16-ounce M-26 Lemon.

"Oh, well... some explosion," replied Harris. "Battlefield details are murky... the fog of war. I understand the surviving squad members are being interrogated so they can piece together what happened."

"I'll tell you exactly what happened," I said quickly. "It was one of the new guys. He got careless loading his suspender rig and accidentally pulled the pin."

"When you're better, soldier, you'll get a chance to give your statement, too."

I want to state it now. "Their first night assignment at a forward bunker, and it was supposed to be the last one for me and Donahue. Please find out if he's okay."

"I don't have any info about your buddy, but I'll make some inquires. I assume he's enlisted."

"Corporal." I patted the blank left sleeve of my hospital gown.

"Hmm. If your buddy's hurt, he ought to be on this ward. I'll ask the nurse on my way out."

"I really need to know, Chaplain. We were both due to rotate back to the world in six days—well, six days from that night duty—March fourteenth. What day is it now?"

"Today is the ninth of March."

We'd gone out before midnight on March seventh, so I'd been out of it for at least one full day—presumably in this hospital, unless I'd already been transferred up the chain. "Which hospital did you say this was?"

"95th Evac," the chaplain answered, "and you're in great hands here."

"Did I come straight here? Or did they take us to a M*A*S*H unit first? Maybe my buddy went somewhere else."

"It's my understanding all the casualties that night came directly here from the fire base and that everybody left together in one Huey."

"Were other bunkers involved?" Then I remembered. It hadn't been an enemy attack. This was *friendly* fire. "Oh, guess not." It finally dawned on me to take a quick inventory... so I felt my crotch, both legs, and my other arm.

Harris chuckled. "You're okay, son. I checked with Doctor Adams before I came over here. All your components are present and accounted for. Just a few cuts and abrasions."

"But my face is covered."

"Like I said, just so your eyes can heal. Or so I was told."

"And I'm not gonna be blind?"

"Remember, the doctors are in charge of that part."

"I need to know about my buddy."

He cleared his throat softly. "Maybe it would make you feel better to tell me a bit about him."

"Me and Donahue are closer than brothers, tighter than twins. We met in basic, went through infantry training together, and shipped over at the same time to the same unit here." Those were our similarities. "But we were also opposites in many ways. He's married, with a daughter... lived in Illinois. I'm single and don't show any signs of changing that any time soon... from Ohio. Donahue loves the Army, craves the structure... he enlisted. I was drafted, kicking and screaming. All that time, people call me Donahue instead of Donague. But my name sounds like *Don-ah-GHEE*. His name is like that singer Troy Donahue."

"Well, soldier, whoever you are. I'm here to provide spiritual comfort if possible."

"You won't get very far with Donahue. For all his faith in our commanders and government that inherited this war, he's a total atheist about God."

"Sorry to hear that. And you?"

"I believe, Chaplain. And in the past I had a lot more faith. But since I've been over here in all this senseless killing and dying... I guess it's rattled my sense of a God who could allow things like this."

"Much of God's master plan will remain a mystery to us in the mortal world, but all will be clear in the afterlife." He paused again and tapped my wrist. "Would you like to have a short prayer before I leave?"

"Like I said, I haven't been very religious here lately, but yeah... I'd be grateful for your prayer, if you're still willing."

It was brief and muttered softly. I couldn't make out many words other than *Lord* and *amen*. "Now I have some other boys to visit. I'll try to check on your buddy. I'll see what I can find out for you, Dona..."

"GHEE. Don-ah-GHEE."

"Okay." He left quickly. Mine must have been the last bed on his rounds, because I didn't hear him visit any other patient on his way out.

SOME TIME PASSED, but I had no idea how long. I dozed now and then. Felt my wrist being handled a few times—pulse being checked, I guess. Was told to swallow some pills once or twice. When I was awake, I could hear movement at nearby beds and occasional moans from other patients. The speaking voices were mostly soft and indecipherable—*must be the medical staff.*

I figured I was on one of the light casualty wards. The guys who were really banged up would probably be tended to elsewhere, so as not to scare the crap out of the rest of us.

I remembered more about the explosion than I'd been able to blurt out to the chaplain...

The forward bunker was about 500 meters out from our perimeter fence and the movement to get there was always harrowing—especially carrying three .50 caliber machine guns and all the extra ammo cans, in addition to our M-16s. Especially with seven newbies. Our sergeant would've never sent us out with that many new kids who'd just arrived in-country—this was all the doing of the butter-bar second looie trying to flex his limp muscles. Corporal Donahue and I were both trying to quiet down the nervous cherries. A few stumbled in the dark over the rough terrain—didn't have their night eyes yet.

It was a relief to get situated in that bunker. So far, so good. One of the newbie privates stumbled into a pile of crap in a corner and cursed—too loudly.

"Keep quiet!" Donahue snapped. "Put an empty ammo crate over that mess. Don't want to dive into it if any bullets head our way."

"How many VC are out there?" asked Newbie A.

"Maybe three, maybe thirty," I replied. "They never leave a forward post empty, but they shift their probing forces from place to place." If I sounded like a veteran, it was because I couldn't even count how many of these assignments I'd drawn in 51 weeks, including at least half that time at Mary Ann. As bad as these listening jobs were, they were nothing compared to patrols in the bush.

One of the cherries looked like he was about to start crying. Fear can do that. So Donahue tried to comfort him. "Look, kid, your rack's in a hooch less than half a mile behind us. This isn't one of those isolated fire bases in spitting distance of the DMZ that's only accessible by chopper. We've got roads back to the nearest town. And a highway to Da Nang... maybe 50 klicks north." Actually Donahue had no idea how many kilometers it was to Da Nang... but his guess made it sound close enough.

"This is nuts," hissed Newbie B. "What are we doing out here?"

"Listening post," I replied, my eyes straining through the darkness toward the distant wire which separated us from the enemy... until they cut through it.

Donahue added more detail. "The ground sensors are supposed to detect movement within 1500 to 4500 meters of our perimeter, but VC sappers seem able to get inside that 1500 meter line from time to time. If you guys will settle down and shut up, we'll monitor any activity in this northeast sector and report back if we hear or see anything. Hopefully it'll be a quiet shift and any probes will be along the other sectors."

"How often does each sector get hit?" asked Newbie C in a shaky whisper.

"They don't post a schedule, idiot," I replied, with no attempt to disguise my impatience. "There's some VC

11

lieutenant way over yonder who spins a wheel three times. Then he sends the probes to those sectors."

"Three probes each night?" asked Newbie D, hunkering down even farther in the bunker.

"Not always. Sometimes no probes," said Donahue, trying—as usual—to calm the cherries. "But it's three more often than any other number. Almost never only one probe, because that would allow us to concentrate our defense and wipe out their patrol. Now settle down and shut up. And keep your heads down. You three on the .50 cal. Everybody else, be sure you load a full magazine in your rifle and have at least two more ready to go from your pouch. You're not gonna like this, but keep those safeties ON. We don't want anybody killed with friendly fire in an American listening post."

"What if the VC come charging in? asked Newbie E, his teeth making a soft chattering noise.

"We'll hear them a long time before they get here and everybody has plenty of time to flick off those safeties," Donahue answered. "The grenades are in a box tucked up here in the front of the bunker where no stray fire can hit them." He'd pointed, but it was so dark, probably nobody saw his gesture. "Quietly, each of you take turns, and grab two... one for each strap of your suspender rig. Got it?"

March 10, 1971

NO IDEA HOW MUCH time had passed when somebody came to the foot of my bed and rustled some papers, probably on the clipboard.

"Who's that?" I asked. *It's amazing how temporary blindness can heighten apprehension.*

"I'm Doctor Adams. Just checking your chart."

"What about my eyes? When do I get these bandages off?"

He had to think for a moment. "Maybe as early as tomorrow morning, soldier. You were lucky. One of the top ophthalmologists in the States just got drafted and rushed through officer orientation. Shipped in-country before he could pin on his gold leaves. He's here this week, making rounds of as many bases as he can fit in. He'll be stationed much further south for his normal tour."

"What did he say?"

"He extracted three tiny slivers—metallic, I think—from your eyes," replied Adams. "Lucky he was here. I couldn't even see what he pulled out. We have him for another day or two and he'll check your eyes tomorrow."

"What about my buddy, Donahue?"

"I thought you were Donahue." He clacked the chart again and tapped the papers.

"I'm Don-ah-GHEE. My buddy is Donahue. Corporal Roger Donahue."

Brief silence except for a piece of paper scraping against cloth, possibly his pocket. The paper was unfolded, probably studied, and then refolded. More sound of paper and cloth.

"I'm sorry, soldier... your buddy didn't make it."

"That can't be!" I felt warm moisture beneath my bandages.

"Sorry, soldier. The casualty list from March eighth, when your whole detail came in, indicates one death. Looks like they spelled it wrong, because this list has two Donahues."

"Everybody's called me Donahue since I got my first buzzcut."

"Well, the records people will straighten it all out. Sorry about your buddy."

I noisily inhaled the contents of my sinuses. "Doesn't make sense. I covered that blast with my helmet under my belly. If anybody died, it should've been me."

After an awkward silence, I heard some whispers. *Somebody else is here.*

"Sometimes the shock of an event like this can confuse things in your mind," said the doctor. "The report I saw indicated that a PFC Donahue took the main impact."

"I'm the PFC, but I'm Don-ah-GHEE. They're always getting us confused. Ever since basic, they've called us both Donahue."

There were more soft whispers. One sounded female.

"Who else is here?"

"The ward nurse is conferring with me, soldier."

No acknowledgement from her.

More whispers and I thought I heard the nurse say the word *corporal.*

13

"I don't know what to tell you, soldier," said Adams. "Your eyes caught a few slivers. Your buddy didn't make it."

"What about the cherries?" I asked, but at that point didn't really care if they'd lived or died.

"All survived, but the ones nearest the blast have injuries. Shrapnel in arms, legs, chest... nothing fatal, with proper care. A few perforated eardrums."

"So the newbie that pulled the pin lives," I muttered, "and my buddy dies? I throw myself on the grenade and get eye slivers... but my buddy dies? That's insane!"

"Settle down, soldier. I'm sorry about your friend. Maybe the chaplain can help you process this."

"He was here earlier." *And not much help, to be honest.*

"Not yet today. Maybe that was yesterday."

"Yesterday?"

"The three chaplains come in around the same time every morning, each going mainly to the guys of their faith, though there's often some overlap. That way we don't have Protestant soldiers laying here without any spiritual comfort while the Catholic and Jewish soldiers are being comforted. Or vice versa."

"How long have I been here? What's the date now?"

"March tenth," replied the nurse in a soft, comforting voice. "You've been here two days so far."

"Thank you, Nurse White." The doctor sounded perturbed. Maybe she wasn't supposed to speak. There was a subdued clank of the metal clipboard. "Well, I have other beds to check."

"Wait, Doc. One more question. Will I have a chance to see my buddy... you know, before they ship him home?"

"Not sure about that, soldier. The mortuary squadron handles all that... or maybe it's the graves registration folks. Not sure. Lots of variables—the flow of casualties, the proportion of mortalities, availability of transport planes. Et cetera." After a pause and a whisper to the nurse, Dr. Adams strode away.

I lay there trying to make sense of how Donahue could've possibly been killed by a blast that only injured my eyes.

Soft footsteps approached my bed. I reached out that direction and a delicate female hand took mine. The nurse had returned. "Are you okay, soldier?" she asked.

"I'll live... apparently. Which is more than I can say for Donahue."

14

No reply, but she tightened her grip on my hand. "If you want to talk about it, I have a minute or two."

"What's your first name, Nurse White?"

"Casey... but I'm not supposed to tell you."

"An officer?"

"Second lieutenant. I'm told I'll get a silver bar when I leave."

"I'm Roy Donague. Pronounced Don-ah-GHEE."

"Don-ah-GHEE," she repeated slowly. It sounded lovely from her. "I heard some of what you said earlier. People always call you Donahue. Easy enough to confuse those names if folks aren't paying attention. My best friend here is Nurse Rhonda Salter... and everybody calls her Nurse Slater."

"Tell her I know how she feels."

"So, you want to talk about your buddy? Sometimes it helps."

Guess I do. But I wasn't sure where to begin. "Donahue's main concern was his wife Jan and their daughter. She hadn't wanted him to enlist, said she was worried he'd get hurt over here."

"Didn't they have a deferment for married guys?" asked Casey.

"All that changed at some point after the first lottery, or so said my buddy. Besides, like Donahue explained it to me, his grandpa went to war, his dad went to war... and in his family, he often told me, the men always answered the call of our country."

"Your friend sounds like a brave and responsible citizen," observed the kind nurse.

"I thought he was nuts... and told him so. But he'd always laugh it off. Sometimes he'd say that I wasn't as cynical, deep down, as I pretended to be."

"Are you?"

"Hard to say." I swallowed hard. "That same question, before the grenade went off, might've had a different answer. Right now, I feel lucky to be alive. I know this—my buddy shouldn't have died. If anybody deserved dying, it was whichever one of those cherries fumbled that grenade pin."

15

THAT NIGHT, I DREAMED—or maybe re-dreamed—the blast. I saw the newbie (though not sure which one) fumble with the grenade handle at his suspender rig strap. The next part seemed like slow motion. The cherry realized the handle had snagged and when he tugged on it, the pin slipped out and fell to the ground. He didn't have enough sense to even say anything... he just stared through the darkness toward the pin, somewhere near his boots presumably, with the live M26 in one hand. Then he flipped it toward one corner of the bunker... as if that would do any of us any good.

Donahue and I both saw everything and for a split-second we looked at each other. I guess it was kind of like me wondering if Donahue was going to do something and him wondering if Donague was. Then the scene sped up to real time—as real as time gets in vivid dreams—and I shoved Donahue's body out of the way before I grabbed my helmet and threw myself on top of the grenade. It wasn't like the movies I'd seen. I didn't even have time to feel any pain—just the instantaneous shock and incredibly loud boom and my belly's innards being blasted through my back. I hadn't had any time to think, "Oh, he's got a wife and kids, so he should live." It was simply instinct kicking in. Live grenade... one close friend and seven cherries on their first detail. If I'd given the matter any rational thought, I'd have tossed two of the newbies on top of that grenade and Donahue and I would both still be short-timers, about two days from the final walk up the ramp to the C-141 taking us back to whichever main base currently handled the commercial flights back to the world.

Then I woke.

It had been a dream, all right... but that's also exactly what happened. So how could Donahue be dead?

☞

March 11, 1971—morning
UNLIKE THE OTHER VISITS from medical staff, when the eye specialist arrived at the foot of my bed, it was with considerable noise and discussion. I recognized the voices of Dr. Adams and Nurse White. There may have been others.

Dr. Clausen—a new major, I remembered hearing before—asked me a few questions, and also consulted both the doctor and nurse about the pills I'd received and whether anyone had

added any additional ointment to my eyes. Then he slowly removed the bandages and checked my eyeballs.

My eyes stung badly—wasn't sure if it was the light or the
air. Maybe both. It was difficult to keep my eyelids open.

"How is your vision now, soldier?" asked Clausen.

"Everything looks cloudy."

"That's the ointment. It's good that you still have that thin
coating because the bandages were supposed to be changed
yesterday and more medicine applied."

I saw clearly enough to know that Adams looked at Casey
and Casey looked back at him. They'd both dropped the ball,
apparently.

"I want at least a week's more treatment for that right
eye," he said. "But I think that single sliver on the left eye was
far enough away from the iris that we'll try to free that one up
in two more days."

"Doc, I'm due to rotate back home on the fourteenth."

"If both eyes are still covered, you're not going anywhere.
You'd be taking up bed space that's needed by a more serious
casualty. But if we get one eye working, they might take you
as walking wounded. I'm new to the military bureaucracy, but
I know the eyes. If you can board that plane with one eye
functioning, they might let you go."

"So there won't be any long-term damage?"

"I see no reason for it. But that partly depends on how good
a patient you are. Some people try to rush the healing, but your
eyes are not replaceable, so give them time to recover."

"Okay, Doc. Thanks."

Then the specialist scribbled on my chart, nodded his
goodbye, and addressed his colleagues. "Anybody else on this
ward?"

"No, Corporal Donahue was the last in your rounds."

"PFC Don-ah-GHEE," I interjected.

With no notice of my correction, the major strode away,
but Adams—who I realized by his railroad tracks was a captain—remained with the nurse, who was sorting out the new
bandages.

"By the way, soldier," said Adams, "I asked about that
mix-up with the names—two Donahues on the casualty page."

We'd been carried that way since basic. "What did they
say?"

"They're still checking with your company's first sergeant."

That didn't fill me with confidence—Charlie Company of the 46th Infantry Battalion was lower on morale than just about any outfit in the 23rd Infantry Division. Most people said it was because *Mary Ann* was so poorly sited along that ridge. Of course, it also could've just been dumb bad luck. Our fire base had components from four other companies in that battalion, along with other detachments. I realized I'd partly tuned out the doctor.

"But they assured me the, um, remains won't ship home until all the records are complete, correct, and verified."

I felt for my own dog tags, but couldn't bring them into focus, not with the film over my eyes. "As long as Jan Donahue gets the correct envelope."

"Is that his mother?" asked Adams.

"His wife. Roger was married with a daughter."

"Hmm. The clerk I spoke to seemed to think Donahue was single."

"This is ridiculous! With as much sloppy detail work as goes on, this army would even screw up R-and-R at a USO show in Japan."

"Easy, soldier. There's a lot going on in-theater. One casualty from a fire base listening post is just as important as 39 Marines killed in a frontal assault near the DMZ. But it takes time to sort out all the information and records. Be patient."

I don't feel patient. There was no reason for Donahue to be dead in the first place. "Doc, can I see him? I mean, before you bandage me back up?"

"Out of the question. We both just got chewed out by the major for not doing something he hadn't even written on the chart. The first few days in-country are tough on these civilian doctors—they're still thinking they have a staff of residents and interns and nurses who are able to read their minds. Doesn't work that way over here." Adams' face looked mildly surprised at how much he'd revealed and he paused abruptly. Clearing his throat, he continued. "Well, anyway, there was a foul-up yesterday so we've got to be certain to follow protocol today."

"I need to see him, Doc. He's my buddy. I have to say goodbye at least."

Nurse White whispered something to the doctor.

18

"Tell you what. The nurse will reapply the ointment and bandages now. And tomorrow after the chaplain comes by, we'll see if we can wrangle a ride in his Jeep over to the morgue. But that's only a maybe."

"With my eyes covered?"

"The nurse will go with you and take off the covering for your left eye." He turned to her to confirm that she agreed. "The major said that eye was already on the mend. A few minutes of exposure shouldn't hurt it any. Then we patch you back up and wait for him to come by again the following day. How does that sound?"

"Risky, for you," I replied. "Are you sticking your neck out?"

He paused. "Soldier, I'm also due to rotate back soon. I've seen a lot of things over here. Sometimes the military red tape and S.O.P. doesn't take into account the human element. I know you're confused about your buddy... and I'm truly sorry he didn't make it. But I also know you're going to need some closure about this experience. And maybe the best way is a couple of minutes face to face with your friend."

"Thanks, Doc." I reached out my hand. "I guess I had you figured wrong."

He smiled, perhaps a bit embarrassed by my compliment, gripped my hand for only a second, and then departed.

"Well, soldier," said Casey, "the standing operating procedure for you right now is more ointment and new bandages."

❧

March 12, 1971—morning
WHEN CHAPLAIN HARRIS returned the following morning, his voice suggested he was in a great mood. He quickly sat and conspiratorially whispered that he'd been briefed by the doctor and nurse and thought our plan was a terrific approach to the closure I needed about my friend. That said, he also cautioned me that the conditions of some battlefield casualties could be quite a shock, especially after four days. "Are you braced for that possibility?"

I'd seen VC bodies at least that old, rotting where they lay. And, of course, I'd seen our own guys—ranging from those hit by a mortar blast that were hardly more than scrambled body parts, to one slender, blond, be-spectacled clerk-type charac-

19

ter whose face had showed only mild surprise, though his chest had been blown open by a sniper round. "Chaplain, I've probably seen one of everything over here, but I'm not going to inspect Donahue's wounds. I just need to say goodbye."

He and Nurse White led me out, helped me into the front seat of the Jeep, and we took off. Riding blind with a chaplain at the wheel was more thrilling than I had imagined—and I mean that in a negative way, since he drove like a lunatic. But we managed to arrive in one piece.

"By the way, soldier," said Harris as his vehicle screeched to a halt, "I wanted you to know they still don't have the names straightened out. The remains they're going to show us are now linked to PFC Don-ah-guu."

"That's Don-ah-GHEE," replied. "The E gets the emphasis, not the U."

No response to my correction.

"Where do we take off the bandage?" asked Casey as we entered a door and what felt like a long, wide hall.

"We're meeting a Sergeant Sprague and he'll take us to a little space they use as a sort of chapel. I've worked with him before, along with others in the mortuary squadron." Then he clutched my elbow and halted me. "Please don't give him a hard time about the name business. When mistakes are made somewhere up the line, the blame sometimes falls on the guys in the morgue. But they're mostly good men and doing their best here. They're not an investigative arm of the unit."

"Okay, Chaplain. I won't hassle this sergeant. But I surely do hope they straighten out things before Donahue is loaded on that transport home."

"I'm sure they will, soldier."

SPRAGUE MET US, ignored me completely, and focused his comments to the chaplain. I assumed he was focusing his visual attention on Nurse White. "When you're ready, Chaplain, I'll escort you to the holding area."

My stomach fluttered with nerves as Casey removed my left eye covering. She peered closely to assess whatever was visible—to her naked eye—of my healing cornea. "Can you see okay, soldier?"

It was a little hazy, and I told her so.

She tilted back my head and administered two drops. After I blinked a few times and she dabbed the extra with a tissue, I could see better.

"How about now?"

"Good to go."

The chaplain opened the door and summoned Sprague, who hurriedly escorted us further into the heart of the morgue facility. Early in my tour I'd had a few beers one night with a lonely-looking morgue private, who warned me it was usually considered bad luck to associate with the dead body corps. But I'd never worried about being jinxed. Anyhow, he'd told me they used generators to chill huge mortuary coolers, so I knew this area would be cold. Wasn't prepared, however, for my very bones to start quaking as I viewed my buddy's body bag.

Standing next to the remains, with both of Casey's hands gripping my left arm, I felt a little faint. My knees didn't actually buckle, but the chaplain also reached out to steady me.

The sergeant whispered a question to Harris, who replied in kind. Then Sprague unzipped the body bag and immediately stepped back two paces.

My left eye was open, but I felt it blink several times. Looking down and expecting the pale face and blond hair of Donahue, the best friend I'd had since busting out of high school... I saw, instead, my *own* face!

The body on that wooden slab table was mine!

There hadn't been any mix-up in the names or identification. The dead guy was PFC Roy Donague—me! *Don-ah-GHEE.*

Without any noise that I can recall, I just sort of melted to the floor. Casey had tried to slow my descent, or at least keep me from conking my head. The chaplain was little help with my collapse, but he quickly went to one knee and begin quizzing me.

"Soldier, are you okay?"

As I heard Sprague zip up the body bag and hurriedly shove away the roller conveyer, I sat—or maybe it was more of a crouch—on the cold cement floor and kept repeating, "That was *me*." Black hair, darker complexion, and a crooked nose. "That was *me*."

"I warned you about a possible shock, soldier," said Harris, in what he likely meant as a soothing voice, "but I had no idea you'd take it this hard. Your friend's remains are in terrific shape, considering. And there was no wounding at all on his face, except his dreadful pale coloring, of course."

"No, no," I said, groaning. "It's not Donahue. That's *my* body."

"Shock," whispered Harris to the nurse. "This was a big mistake. Let's get this boy back to the ward."

MERCIFULLY, THE RIDE BACK was slow and uneventful. Nothing more was said by either the chaplain or the nurse. Once they got me back inside and Casey helped me out of my fatigues, I found myself in bed again. Not sure of the correct terminology, but certainly I was dazed.

Harris tried to comfort me. "It's probably the shock. The mind plays tricks after trauma. Things will sort themselves out later." To Casey, he whispered a question about a possible sedative.

She whispered back that they'd have to clear it with the doctor on duty.

"I'm sorry, soldier," said Harris, turning his attention back to me. "I really thought it would help. Closure, you know." Then he instructed the nurse to put the patch back on my eye... and he left.

Looking worried and a bit rattled herself, Nurse White had gathered what was needed and was about to re-bandage my left eye.

"Wait, Casey. Give me a couple more minutes. I need to see your face when I explain this." I gulped thickly. "That was *me*. That long, black bag held *my* body. I'm not crazy... and I can prove it."

"Settle down, soldier," she said, placing her tape and gauze on the bed's surface. "You've been through a lot. Your vision is probably still a little cloudy."

"I can see *you*."

"How well?"

"Perfectly."

She slid the chair closer and sat down. "Let's check that perfect vision, soldier. What do you see?"

"Trim and athletic-looking, tall for a girl, cute figure... short brown hair and blue eyes, with dimples on a very pretty face. Isn't that you?"

"Well, you flatter me in some details, but, yes, you've accurately described my appearance. Let's see how good your eyes are at distance and counting. How many empty beds on this ward?"

I stretched my neck and turned my torso. "None. They're all full."

"Okay, soldier, that was test number two. Number three: how many total beds in this ward?"

I counted the row across the wide aisle and doubled it. "Including mine, there's 32. Unless there's a bed behind that curtain in the corner."

"No, that curtain is portable. And your count is correct— 32 patients and they're all mine, for the next hour and a half. So I have 31 other guys to check on. Your vision is A-OK. Now let me put in this cream and we'll get the bandage back in place. That specialist wants total non-use for your eyes to heal."

"Wait, Casey, before you cover my eye back up. Tell me one more thing. How do *I* look?"

"When we were standing together earlier, you were several inches taller than me, so I'd guess maybe six-one. Blue eyes, blond hair, and a look," she said, blushing slightly, "that most women would consider classically handsome."

"That's Donahue!" I reached for her hand, which she quickly retracted. "I'm about five-ten with black hair, dark complexion, brown eyes, and a crooked nose." I looked to the beds nearest me and saw most of those patients staring. "That proves it. You just described my buddy and I just saw *my* body at the morgue."

"Calm down, soldier. You're upsetting my other patients."

"Don't you believe your own eyes, Casey?"

She shook her head. "I told you what I see. And I'm sorry to repeat this, but your friend will soon be loaded on that mortuary plane, headed back to the world."

"No, I'm telling you that was my body... and this is Donahue's."

"Settle down. Like the chaplain said, even if your vision checks out okay, your mind can still play tricks." She fingered the gauze and tape. "Now let's wrap up that eye socket."

"No. Wait. You were there. You got a pretty good look at that body, didn't you?"

She sighed heavily. "At that point, I was focused more on you... my *live* patient."

"And the face was completely intact, since the blast was down around the upper belly and blew out the back."

"Well, I didn't see the wound area."

Staring into her face, I detected a strange expression. "Doesn't matter. You saw the face. I know you did. Now tell me what you saw."

She started to rise from the chair. "Soldier, I've got other patients..."

"Tell me... please."

Settling back in her seat, she said, softly and haltingly, "Dark hair, Roman nose, and his original coloring would have been sort of Mediterranean, I guess."

"Me!" I slapped my own chest. "We get the coloring from my mom's side—Italian."

She rubbed her temples. "Now you're confusing me, soldier."

"Like I told you folks before, I was the one on top of the grenade. The blast *killed* me. Donahue escaped with scratched eyeballs, plus a few nicks and abrasions... but the guy in the body bag is *me*." I studied her for a reaction, but didn't see any. "Just like people always getting our names fouled up... but now they've got the bodies switched."

She reached to the foot of my bed. "This chart belongs to Corporal Roger Donahue, who—as we've just clarified—is tall, blond, light-complected, with blue eyes. The chart was matched to your dog tags when you were brought in."

"There's a big mistake here, Casey."

"Look, soldier. Maybe my powers of description are not all that great. We work six days straight, I've been on duty for nearly eleven hours today, and I need a break. Forget how I described your features. Things will be better tomorrow. In another day your left bandage comes off for good and you'll be out of here with only your right eye covered. Now let me apply that cream."

"Wait... please. Don't turn out my lights until we settle this. I need to see myself."

"Come on, soldier. You're not my only patient."

"Have you got a mirror? Ten seconds is all I ask. Something's crazy and it's not me suffering from blast trauma. That was my body in the mortuary and you just described my *bud-dy's* face when you looked at me. Let me see a mirror."

While folding her arms in a classically reluctant pose, she also eyed her watch. Then, after a pause, said, "We don't keep mirrors on the ward. Some of the troops that come through here don't need to be seeing the damage to their faces."

"Please."

"Oh, all right. Hold on. I think there's a makeup compact in the desk at the nurse's station."

"That'll do. Thanks."

She was gone for less than a minute. "Now promise me, after you look, you'll settle down and forget all this crazy talk about switched bodies."

I nodded but didn't promise... because I already knew who was in that mirror. Taking a deep breath, I opened the compact—and saw the face of Corporal Roger Donahue.

∽

March 13, 1971—morning
A LOT HAPPENED THE following morning.

Early on, the eye specialist returned, un-bandaged and examined both eyes, then replenished the filmy ointment in my right eye and switched to clear drops for my left. His verdict was still out for my right, but Dr. Clausen pronounced my left eye's vision as fine, though especially sensitive to light. That might or might not be temporary, he said. That eye needed one more day under the bandage.

Chaplain Harris also returned, and again apologized for what he now characterized as the ill-fated trip to the mortuary the previous day.

During Dr. Adams' subsequent visit, I was informed I *would* be allowed to rotate stateside on my normal date, March fourteenth... tomorrow. And among my first set of appointments at Travis AFB in-processing was meeting the eye specialist there.

I'd told all three of them that I was Donague now living inside Donahue's body, but none of them commented about it further—at least not to me. Adams did tell me that he'd referred me to a psychiatrist at Travis, and he made it clear this was not just the routine interview where they're checking off a box while processing your transition forms.

25

As Adams left my bedside, he whispered his conclusion (to the nurse) that I was suffering from some sort of transference delusion, where the trauma of losing a friend added to the guilt that I hadn't taken action myself. And all that had somehow convinced me that I was him—the actual dead guy. Of course he had it perfectly backwards. I *had* taken action and I'd died from the blast... but now I was somehow inside Donahue's body.

"But he saw the body," replied Casey in an equally low whisper.

"Fog of war, nurse. The mind mis-translates what the eyes take in."

⌒

LATER THAT MORNING, I heard Nurse White back at my bedside.

"Doc doesn't believe me, Casey."

"What?"

"Just because my eyes are bandaged doesn't mean I'm also deaf. I heard what he told you earlier."

She patted my hand and straightened the bed sheet without comment.

"It's okay that he doesn't believe me... but do you?"

The nearby chair squeaked as its feet scraped the industrial tile flooring. I heard Casey sit and then scoot closer to the bed. "Soldier, I know you've been through a lot. Being temporarily without your sight certainly complicates your resumption of, um, normalcy. I do believe that you truly think you saw your own body in that mortuary bag."

"So you think I'm nuts."

No reply.

"That was me in the morgue yesterday. My face. I ought to know it. It's been with me for twenty years and I've shaved it almost every day for the last five. Donahue's face is totally different. That's one of the reasons that we griped so much about our names being continually confused—we look like opposites."

Checking her watch, White patted my hand, rose from the chair, and hurried to her next patient.

⌒

March 14, 1971—morning
A NEW DAY DAWNED—my departure from Southeast Asia and my return to the world. I greeted that long-awaited day with

26

my left eye finally uncovered (presumably for good) and dressed in my Class A uniform for travel.

"Well, you've got your marching orders," said Nurse White with a sad-looking smile. "As of this morning, you're discharged from our medical care... and after a few hours of expedited out-processing, you should be on board the transport."

"Casey, I wish there was some way I could spend more time with you... you know, outside the hospital."

After a long silence, she replied, "Hear me out before you interrupt." She swallowed hard. "For every ten patients we nurses see, there are two who want to have a drink with us, another two who want to date us, and there's usually at least one who thinks we should marry."

"What about the other five?"

"Don't interrupt. That's one of several reasons I shouldn't have told you my first name. The nurse-patient relationship has an intimate feel to it, but it's not a relationship of the other kind. And those few people who do take it farther together usually realize pretty quickly that nurse and patient is not a great basis for marriage... certainly not for people at such a young age. You're a good soldier, and—I believe—a kind soul. And you have a wife and child at home waiting for you."

"Those are Donahue's people. I've never even met them. I can't go home in Donahue's body and live with his family. His wife will immediately know that I'm different from the Donahue she kissed goodbye at Travis a year ago."

"Soldier, everybody's different when they rotate home. Southeast Asia changes a person, no matter what role they played here. But for the guys who've experienced combat, it's understandably more profound. Travis, or whatever base you're returning to, will have held at least a couple of sessions with each wife who's expecting a husband back soon. They're braced to expect changes, moods, anxiety, and so on."

"But not a completely different person."

"There are lots of adjustments. You'll probably have a new assignment. Depending on how much time is left in your enlistment, you may be transferred to a new base, with new quarters, different school for your daughter, and so on."

"His daughter. And we both enlisted the same day, but in different places—him in Carbondale, Illinois, and me in Sandusky, Ohio."

"I assume you'll get out when your hitch is up."

"I certainly plan to... and good riddance to the Army. But Donahue was actually talking about re-upping."

"Soldier, you keep talking about two different people. But one person left two days ago in a body bag—sorry to put it so bluntly—and you're soon heading home to a family. I don't know what it will take... maybe counseling... but you need to resolve things sufficiently to live one life with one identity."

I sat there on the edge of my hospital bed, wondering if any other person had ever faced the prospect of living his remaining years in someone else's body. "We were close... brothers, buddies forever, whatever you call it. But I never imagined we'd be so close that we'd become a single person."

There was a lengthy pause before she replied. "Along with everything you two shared together—from day one in boot camp through the night of the incident—you've clearly admired your friend. You've looked up to him for his sense of responsibility and dedication."

"So you do believe me! You realize I'm Donague suddenly living in Donahue's body."

She smiled cautiously. "Soldier, I've seen crazy things over here. How could I rule out your, um, situation? Remembering that you were leaving today, I got to thinking last night. I heard you tell the chaplain that your friend was basically an atheist, whereas you're a man of some faith, however undeveloped. I doubt Chaplain Harris would endorse this, but what if that spiritual PFC who threw himself on the grenade to save the others... somehow *deserved* another chance at complete redemption?"

"That sounds like a script for an old Hollywood movie."

"You don't consider it possible that the Divine Plan—whatever it may be—has room for a few do-overs?"

"All the grunts I know over here have a pretty fatalistic view of things—if your number comes up, you're gone... period."

She nodded. "Yeah, I've noticed there's not an excess of hope over here. I think that's one reason the friendships here can become so deep—like you and your buddy."

Now I smiled. "There were times, when Donahue would talk about his wife and daughter in Carbondale, that I thought I wanted to *be* him."

"And now's your opportunity." She shoved back her chair and stood to leave.

"Wait, Casey. One more thing." I gulped. "Are you absolutely positive there's no chance of anything ever happening between you and me?"

"Soldier, like I already explained: we get love notes, propositions, and proposals—not to mention randy creeps with roving hands. I like you, but you're one patient out of thousands I'll see by the time I rotate home."

"What's your E.O.T.?"

"My end of tour is May 30—eleven weeks from yesterday."

"So there's no chance..."

"Soldier, I had a life before I shipped out. I was dating a guy back home. We've kept up correspondence and there's a strong possibility we'll pick things back up."

"So there's no conceivable way for me to go home as PFC Donague... the guy I really am. And apparently no real reason for me to even want to."

"Your paperwork, your rank, your belongings—not to mention your face and body—all identify you as Corporal Donahue."

I'd forgotten my few belongings in our hooch. "You mean they shipped away my stuff?"

She nodded slowly. "In most cases, all they ship home are the few personal items... like letters, photos, and such. Any other items—especially dirty pictures—are discarded."

"So there's nothing left of me—Donague—except my mind and soul." *And memories.*

"And heart." She pointed. "Make room in there for that wife and child. Do what you can to honor your friend by living out his obligations."

"I thought I was sacrificing a lot when I threw myself on that grenade. Now I have to sacrifice again? More?"

"If things are as you believe, then you're the rare individual who gets a second chance. It'll be an adjustment to experience that life in different circumstances, but think of all the good you can accomplish." She straightened her O.D. green uniform and started to leave. "Goodbye, soldier, and good luck."

"Casey, wait. Will you do one more thing before you leave?"

She waited, her eyebrows arched. She'd probably been asked for hundreds of kisses or hugs.

"Just say my name, my real name. I'd like to hear it one more time before PFC Donague ceases to exist, except in my own mind."

"You want to hear me say your name?"

"Please. I've been in this man's army for 31 months and I doubt I've heard my correct name from anybody except Donahue. Say it once, and I won't bother you any more. Say it slow, so I can hear you perfectly."

"Very well." She patted my hand softly. "Good luck and goodbye, Don-ah-GHEE."

END

A Lousy Way to Rye

Charles A. Salter

THE WORST DAY OF my life began as I noticed my left arm falling off.

Luckily it wasn't my dominant one. The right brushes my teeth, combs my hair, and wipes my ass. But the left had been important, too. It used to help hold the dental floss, pull back hair to expose my part, and tug the left butt cheek out of the way of the roving TP. I was going to miss that arm.

And I would make him pay for doing this to me.

But how?—when my mind kept playing tricks and I wasn't even sure who I was any more, nor where I was, nor why. I needed hints like Guy Pearce in *Memento*. *Have I had the presence of mind to store hints, reminders to steer me through the disintegration?*

I checked my pockets. Full of something.

The first thing I pulled out was an ID for a Mack Drane. Was that image of me? I looked at my dim reflection in the window of the trailer, and it looked like a possible match. Maybe. If I was Drane, then I had a sudden moment of clarity about what I must have been doing before the attack that left me in a suffocating mental fog:

A counter-terrorism expert working out of Fort Detrick, Maryland, Drane had been stalking an extremist for days, hoping to trace him to his stash of biological weapons. Drane and team had found the mobile roving laboratory secreted in a STAA double pup tractor trailer, parked at the Maryland House rest stop on I-95 near Aberdeen. Hidden in plain sight, passed by thousands of cars an hour.

Dressed in full Biosafety Level 4 biocontainment garb, the experts had searched the rear pup and found the ergot tanks, each filled with moist and rotting rye grains, sprouting enough mycotoxin from the *Claviceps purpurea* fungus to destroy every living thing in a small town.

The forward pup held his testing cages... along with their dead occupants—a few cats, a couple of dogs, and some young human migrants likely smuggled across the border by coyotes and sold for a double profit.

All had expired and were putrefied, their bodies betraying the signs of ergotoxicosis. Feet and hands rotted away with gangrene, the limbs twisted into once-agonizing rigidity by the convulsions. Large, swollen sores riddled the skin all over. Cages filled with diarrhea and vomit. In my mind I could see how awful their final moments must have been, imagining them hallucinating, beating their heads against the bars to stifle the excruciating headaches.

Not hard to imagine, since it was now happening to me. First nausea and intestinal distress, tingling alternating with numbness all over, periodic spasms, the beginnings of paranoia and hallucinations, the loss of my arm. Somehow he'd gotten to me when I hadn't been protected by my garb. Either that or he'd corrupted my suit, or had devised a terrifying new variant of the fungus that could penetrate even the highest level of biocontainment.

Somehow.

And he was going to pay, this terrorist. What was his name? Ah, yes, Zevlin Neruder, the one being tracked throughout the U.S. northeast for days. I didn't know how much time I had left, but I would make him pay.

Oh, yeah, we were going to catch up with Zevlin Neruder, and when we did, I wasn't planning on an arrest.

A young man in Biosafety Level 4 garb emerged from the trailer. *Who's this? Friend or foe?* I reached into my pocket again and pulled out a sheaf of small notes written on scraps of paper—gambling markers, a couple of addresses, a list with but three names, FBI Special Agents Frank Chalmers, Brice Cannon, and Ryan Kaputnik.

"Boss, you gotta see this," said the man as a slip of paper fell from his hand. "Oops," he grunted.

"Chalmers? What is it?"

He bent over to retrieve it as I hurriedly sought for more clues in my pocket. More gambling markers... was I a gambler? A personal photo of a gorgeous woman; written on the back was "With love, Mary Beth." My girlfriend? Wife? Or that of my enemy? Oh, yeah, Drane's girlfriend. She didn't know anything about the secret plot, but she knew Drane was zeroing in on some big anti-terrorism score. That made her a perfect bargaining chip for Zevlin Neruder.

The man stood up after kneeling on the floor to retrieve something.

"What is it?" I asked again. Apparently he hadn't heard me the first time.

"A gas receipt."

"From here?"

"No, you'll never believe it."

"C'mon, dummy. Time is fleeting."

"The station in New Market next to where Mary Beth Nighthaven lives."

My heart missed a tap then hit the drum twice in a row to catch up. Mary Beth in danger, too? *He must know all about me and wants to get me and mine before I get him.*

"Let's go," I told him.

"Are you sure, boss? You don't look so good."

"And where's Brice?"

"He's dead, boss. You know that. What's the matter with you? Did you get a dose when we opened those tanks?"

"We've got to get to Mary Beth's before it's too late."

"But what about your arm?"

I picked it up and wobbled dizzily to the nearby HAZMAT truck, nestled my own dead flesh carefully within a portable freezer among the tissue samples taken for later lab analysis. "They can pick up the truck later. We'll take the car. You drive, Bubba. I'm not myself today."

"Is that some kind of joke, boss?"

"Just drive." The Dodge Charger SRT-8 with 250 bhp engine sped out of the parking lot with squealing tires.

The acceleration made me dizzy, set my tingling and frayed neurons on fire. The jackhammer of a headache wouldn't let up. I tried to distract myself by taking in the scenery. But the trees in the background seemed to melt as we neared them, merging into a blurry slag of green. I closed my eyes to keep from blowing that morning's grapefruit, grape nuts, and seedless grapes all over the car. A perfect, healthy grape breakfast. The grapiest of grapy sooper-dooper breakfasts... but only healthy if I could keep it down.

My driver sounded worried. "Time for the hospital, boss? Let me get you an ambulance, and I can take care of Mary Beth for you."

I looked at him through unfocused eyes. He seemed to be sprouting whiskers and skin keratoses as large as weeds. "No. The hospital won't be much use at this point, but I can take care of Marcy Beth before I completely lose my mind."

"I thought it was Mary."

"What I said—Mary Beth." Just before I closed my eyes again, it seemed as if my driver was sprouting antennae. Like a roach. Metamorphosis. Kafka.

When will I lose so much of my mind that I no longer realize I am losing my mind? Can I get the job done before I forget what it is? Damn that Zevlin Neruder and his biowarfare toxins. How in hell did he breach my Biosafety Level 4 containment suit, anyway? Must have punched one or more holes in my suit that were too small to see. But when? How? No one has handled my suit but me and—

"Ryan?"

"Yeah, boss?"

"You know Zevlin Neruder, right?"

"Of course." He snickered. "Why wouldn't I?"

"How well do you know him?"

"As well as anyone. As well as *you*." He snickered again. "What are you getting at, anyway?"

His voice sounded like deep, bass echoes from a living mummy's steps in an open sepulcher. Like a voice from the beyond, triggering a second jackhammer in my exploding skull.

"You and I were the only ones handling my suit and yours. Yet here I am dying of ergotoxicosis and you seem fine." *He doesn't really seem fine. He seems to be turning into some kind of beetle.* I looked down at my own forearm, the only one left... at the growing, oozing sores, and wondered when that arm might fall off, too.

"Good point, boss. I've been wondering about that. We both worked that mobile lab for the past three days. But I'm fine... so far."

No, you're not... you're turning into a giant insect... or maybe a monster from outer space.

"And there's something else I don't get," he continued. "With your left arm gone, why aren't you bleeding to death?"

"The fungal poison killed that arm to begin with by constricting its blood flow. The vessels have pretty much shut down and are barely leaking." I looked down at my left shoulder, starting to reek now of gangrene, and confirmed there was not much more than a red ooze staining my tee and the beige leatherette car seat.

I looked out the window. The background palette of green trees and shrubs, grimy buildings and paved roads, blackened telephone poles and overhead, pigeon-stained wires was melting together like the pastels of a watercolor painting left outdoors in the cold September rain.

He pulled off Interstate 70 West at 75 North and entered New Market. "Coming up on Mary Beth's house, boss. Get ready. I see her regular car, but there's another car I've never seen before just a bit down from the driveway."

"Marcy Beth," I corrected.

"Mary."

"Okay, Mary. What are we doing here?"

"You wanted to rush over and take care of her. Remember, boss? Are you sure you're up to this? You look half dead to me. You really need a doctor."

I shook my head. It felt heavy, as if my hair had turned to thick fibers of lead. "Who does the other car belong to, do you think?" I asked.

"An enemy, I'll wager."

Wager. I am a gambler. I like to gamble. At least until I lost a fortune in Atlantic City. Maybe that's when my troubles started. I owed them big time. I was looking at an agonizing date with the sharks if I couldn't pay up. But they said if I did exactly what they wanted it would all go away. I could get my markers back, tear 'em up, flush 'em down de commode, and be free. FREE—yeah!

"Should I park right up front or back at our usual observation point?"

"Up front. We can get in faster that way." *Gambling. Isn't everything in life a gamble? You wake up, dress, and leave the house, and it's like pressing down the arm on the slot machine.*

35

Maybe you'll lose it all... maybe win something... maybe lose your arm and die from ergot poisoning... this gamble to pay off my debts turned me into a one-armed bandit, didn't it?

My driver slammed the brakes at the top of her driveway and I jumped out, pulling my .357 Magnum revolver from its holster. Colt and Wesson Model 66.

"You stay here and keep an eye out for any other intruders. I got this."

Dashing for the front door, I remembered the place now. It used to be a friendly bungalow nestled among some small pine and oak trees. Now it seemed to be growing, like a lava castle atop an expanding volcanic cone. Did my girlfriend live here or did an evil Grimm Brothers witch? Would she lure me in with gingerbread, shoot me dead, or welcome me with open arms? Would my missing arm terrify her or turn her on?

The door was unlocked. I threw it open and burst in, my four-inch pistol barrel pointed forward at eye level, ready to burn to ash any gingerbread man who didn't belong.

She stood at the oven range in the kitchen, her hour-glass-shaped back to me. Tall, thin, with long cascading brown hair. Wearing that sky blue apron I loved that read "Kiss me, stupid." She turned as she responded to the sound. Her once pretty face shocked me. Looked now like an unwashed iron frying pan, with slits for eyes and a freaky Halloween pumpkin mouth.

She screamed, "Zevlin Neruder!"

"Where?" I whirled around and saw a gingerbreaded terrorist looming over us both, as tall as the ceiling, but soft and doughy, uncooked, reaching out to envelop and smother us in waves of gooey dough. I blasted away, downing him with three 158-grain slugs from my Combat Magnum. The first roaring blast singed my cochlea hairs, crapping up my hearing, but the final two sounded like faint echoes from a massive cliff far away. Maybe the white cliffs of Dover.

I leapt back to avoid the collapsing pile of soft pastry dough man and bumped into Marcy Beth.

She screamed again. "Don't hurt me!" She buried her frying pan face into two hands that looked like sauce pans, a doublet of dirty ones all encrusted with grime as if they had barbecued half a hog and hadn't been washed since.

"He'll never be able to hurt you ever again. Not never again."

She took two steps back from me. "You've lost an arm!"

"Not really. I know exactly where it is."

I stepped forward to hug her with my one good arm. "It's okay. You can kiss me now. I'm 'Stupid'."

She recoiled again.

My driver's voice at the door. "Boss, we've got to get out of here! There's a bunch more guys coming!"

I glared at the man-sized Kafka cockroach standing in the doorway, the carapace glistening cool and black in the red glow of twilight. "I thought I told you to stay put!"

"I did... until I was outmanned and outgunned. We've got to git right now, or this will be our Alamo."

"You mean our final Bolivian shootout."

"What?"

I warily slipped along the wall towards him, eyes on possible danger sneaking forward from outside.

Bullets rang out and whizzed past my ears. *FBI revolvers, I'll wager; not the SWAT team's sniper rifles.*

He slammed the door and dove for the floor, extracting his Browning 9mm pistol as he hit the hardwood maple-veneer tiles. He crept towards the steaming kitchen as shattered window glass ripped through the air, exploding like the billions of shards after the Hiroshima nuke hit Japan.

I knelt down and glanced at every window I could see, trying to assess the current threat outside. Couldn't see anything clearly. Everything as musty as when having no glasses and eyes shut at a funeral...

He now sat on the kitchen floor with his back to the inner wall. "Mary Beth is dead, boss. What happened?"

"I dunno. I guess one from that last volley must have hit her."

I sat on the floor with my back to the wall, too. *What happened to the dough boy? All those shots fired, and now there is only one body I can see, Mary Marcy's. Where did the gingerbread man go?*

"We're done for, boss. There's too many of them."

"Not if you can reach those ammo packs on our burro. Then we can make a run for it to Australia."

"What the hell you talkin' about, man?"

37

I looked at Ryan Butch Cassidy and wondered why he didn't get the drift of my Sundance Boss.

Why am I here? What is my mission? Have I completed it? Everything was blurring together now, past, present, and future. *Not much future left, I reckon.* Unless Sundance can get to the ammunition on our burro. *If Butch can cover for him... no, that's not right. I can cover for him, but he can't cover for me. I've got to do the fancy shooting while he runs for the ammo.*

Plan resolved. *We'll make it to Australia yet.*

As I struggled to my feet, my surviving arm convulsed and the pistol accidentally went off. The bullet exploded through Butch's forehead, and his Browning slipped from his limp fingers, clattering to the floor, soon covered by a spray of red and bits of grey matter.

I flung open the front door and leapt through, shooting dozens of times in all directions, at everything that moved, without stopping to reload. An endless six-shot revolver that never ran out. Or was I just clicking on empty? *Whatever. Gotta get to that burro.*

A guy dressed like Popeye the sailor man, toot, toot! No, not that uniform... some kinda uniform, different one... tackled me. Strong, must eat his spinach.

He handcuffed my right wrist to my belt behind my back. Then forced me into a stand. My burro fled at the sight of defeat. No Australia now.

"This is Special Agent Frank Chalmers of the FBI. I arrest you, Zevlin Neruder, for the murders of CID Agent Mack Drane and loan shark Brice Cannon, and for conspiracy to commit bioterrorism."

Just then my second arm fell off and dangled from my belt via the handcuffs, and I puked out what remained of my feeble guts.

Like I said, the worst day of my life...

END

As His Excellency Wishes

J. L. Salter

August 1988—Friday

"I DON'T THINK I can stand another social event with your office people," I said, though trying for sympathy rather than complaining for its own sake.

"It's not much to ask," replied my younger wife, "just show up and smile a bit. You needn't converse beyond the usual greetings unless you want to."

"I scarcely know the language, Yvonne. There was such a rush to get over here that I had no time..."

She dismissed my chronic gripe with a wave of her manicured hand. "I was able to manage, dear." Then she smiled... the cool smile that was more for cocktail parties than for husbands. "We've gone over all this before. The money over here is nearly three times what I could make in the States."

"Yeah, for your position." Yvonne was one of three associate directors to the chief of the entire education department for that small country. "But not for mine." My position was hardly more than a non-tenured college instructor, non-tenured because the entire contract was only for three years... subject to renewal by the chief.

"Your salary here is also considerably more than back home, Larry. But we couldn't make it what you'd hoped for because it would've had the odor of nepotism."

We were about eight months into this contract and it would be nearly another ten months before we could have our single six-week furlough back to the States. I couldn't wait— I'd been miserable the whole time... including the months leading up to our travel here. I was currently 41 but could

39

easily be mistaken for 50—the stress of feeling out-of-place had thinned my hair and thickened my belly.

"Besides," added Yvonne after I'd given no reply, "this position is superb for my career." She was not yet 38 and could pass for 30—this contract and its high level position had invigorated her. "Even if we don't renew, I can probably go back home to my choice of jobs in the federal education department... maybe even in the cabinet-level offices of the Secretary."

I just nodded. I had no desire to live and work in the D.C. area, either. But it would be a whole lot better than this unsettled place, where some massive change always seemed to be brewing. "Aren't you ever worried about the shaky government here?" I asked. It was also rumored to be incredibly corrupt.

"This country is starving for education," she replied. "No matter who's in the top executive positions, these citizens need comprehensive literacy and a structured learning program. And that's what we're doing." Yvonne paused to admire a set of earrings I didn't recognize... before putting them on. "Besides, over here, we have a free hand—well, almost—in doing whatever is needed to bring their existing education efforts up to snuff. Almost unlimited resources."

Yes, that had been the draw, when Yvonne had first spotted the full-page ads in the *Chronicle of Higher Education*. Fantastic salaries and benefits, free luxurious housing within the walls of the presidential compound, and unlimited resources. Plus the opportunity and challenge of going over with the energetic first wave of new blood—North American blood.

"So let's get on to this event. We won't even need the car." Then she pointed to my tie, apparently not up to snuff. "And do make an effort, dear."

THE PARTY HAD BEEN a bust... for me, anyway. Though Yvonne seemed to enjoy herself in this, and comparable, societal situations. She had a great deal more social ease than I possessed. Plus, she seemed to know so many more of these individuals—with their un-spellable names and unfathomable language. In particular, with that new gown she said had arrived from Paris, she'd attracted a lot of attention from the male attendees. I couldn't tell a Parisian dress from one stitched together in New Jersey, but she explained it was just another of the numerous perks of this contract.

I had mainly sipped an overly sour martini and drifted toward the luxurious sofas along the wall of the suite at the disposal of the department's director, Frank. He was elegant and handsome, for a man of about 60. He'd left a job as president of a small but prestigious American university to take the position. On the few occasions he and I had spoken, he'd said much the same things my wife often repeated: it was the opportunity of a lifetime, with fantastic salary, plentiful allowances, and unlimited resources for the department. Apparently, most of the resource-rich countries of the world had considerably more leeway than America in governing and budgeting. If this government wanted something done, they could hire the best and brightest and give them everything needed to get the job done. Quite unlike the American system of public bids, EPA approvals, permits at every level, disclosures, auditors, et cetera. And if anybody ever challenged the government's initiatives, they might receive a call—or, more chillingly, a visit—from the rat-faced chief of internal state security, Mr. Raphael.

I'd been on the couch for much of the evening before I engaged one of the other spouses, who were also little more than ornamentation for the principals at this office party. Like me, Anita was a mere instructor at the state-run university, though I couldn't recall which department... and, at that point of the evening, I didn't care to inquire. Anita looked, however, about as miserable as I felt.

The only highlight of the evening came after most of the other guests had departed, when Frank ushered into his office Yvonne and the two other associate directors. In what seemed an oversight, Frank reopened his office door and beckoned for his mousy wife, me, Anita, and the other spouse.

I'd never seen inside the director's study before. *Wow.* It was an office to die for. Elegance and opulence—though far more tasteful (to my eye, anyway) than the offices of the high-ranking local administrators. As Frank was making some introductory remarks, I looked over my right shoulder at a television which was on, though at a low volume. I was fiddling with the buttons, trying to turn off the distracting TV just at the moment Frank blurted out his announcement of the gen-

erous bonuses he'd obtained for his three loyal subordinates...
and no doubt for himself as well. Each bonus was more than
I'd make in a year back in the States.

"Are you more interested in my office television than in
your wife's bonus?" asked Frank pointedly. Others—except
Yvonne, of course—tittered politely. Frank's wife, whose name
I didn't even know, just stared with a glazed expression.

I blushed as I sputtered my explanation... before I realized
Frank already knew I was merely trying to eliminate the dis-
tracting noise. But it had suited him to embarrass me anyway.
Nice chap.

IT WAS MOSTLY SILENCE on the short walk back to our excellent-
ly appointed, state-provided quarters. I could tell Yvonne was
upset with me, even though I'd done nothing except had the
bad luck to be the person nearest the distracting TV.

"I think I missed the beginning of Frank's announcement,"
I said tentatively. "This isn't a holiday that I know of. Why the
big bonus check?"

"We've completed the planning and equipping of the start-
up for the totally overhauled educational system. Plus, we
have most of the teachers already re-trained. Frank was celebrating our hard work and success at getting it done in only
eight months. Back in the States—if it had even been ap-
proved—this would have taken two years or more."

I remembered now... she'd mentioned their progress. "In
other words, way ahead of schedule."

Yvonne nodded, with the smile of an advertising executive
who'd just signed a huge national contract. "And starting Monday, we launch the new curriculum in all the schools that are
open, and at least ninety percent of the classrooms in each."

"You three and the boss have made a good team, it
seems," I observed.

When Yvonne nodded, it felt like she held back a comment. I wondered if it related to Melissa, who my wife had always considered the weakest member of the associate director
triad.

"You do understand I was only turning off the TV so we
could all focus on what Frank was saying." It was both a
statement and a question.

Again, she only nodded.

⌒∽⌒

August 1988—Saturday

I'D HEARD LOUD noises overnight, but couldn't figure out where they'd come from. Must have been from beyond the walls of the massive presidential compound, where we resided. On rising, I turned on the state-run television but found only static on both channels. Entering the kitchen, I saw Yvonne staring out the window toward the compound's south wall. "Did you hear any loud noise last night?"

She waved me silent. When Yvonne turned, I saw she had the wall phone to her ear. I hadn't noticed the cord curling around the arched doorway from the living space.

I stood behind her and also looked out the window, but saw nothing out of the ordinary besides a few distant areas of smoke. Fires were not common in the neighborhoods outside the compound perimeter, but they did not seem indicative of much besides people burning trash, or whatever the locals did outside the vast compound.

Yvonne said goodbye to whoever was on the line and then walked around the archway to hang up the phone. "I've been on the phone all morning," she said, without explanation.

I hadn't heard the phone ring.

She evidently caught my thought. "Didn't want to wake you, so I dialed some of the calls myself."

"What about? What's going on?"

"It's about the president."

"Of America?"

"No, here. President Diego."

I'd never even seen him in person. "Is he ill?"

"Worse than that," she said with a bit of glaze over her eyes. "He's been replaced."

"Replaced?" I wasn't up on the local language and didn't follow politics to speak of, but I hadn't heard of any election over here. "So who won?"

"Are you familiar with Colonel Ortiz?"

I squinted to help my memory. "I've seen him on TV a lot recently, but never understood what was going on. Did he win the election?"

"It wasn't actually an election."

Oh, crap. That meant it had been another coup. "So what happened to Diego?"

"Not sure. Some say he made it out of the country and found refuge with a neighbor in the region who's also a distant relative. Some say he flew to the States in a private jet."

I thought it was more likely that Mr. Raphael had him down in a dungeon somewhere, but I kept quiet. "So will this new president let your group continue with these educational reforms?"

She nodded. "That's one of the good results. President Ortiz seems every bit as supportive of education as Diego was."

"So your team," meaning Frank and top three who'd been in his study last night, "are still good to go?"

"As with nearly every regime change, there's the possibility of some, uh, realignments at the department levels."

"This doesn't jeopardize your fat bonus check, does it?"

"We'll know on Monday when I deposit it, but I think that's safe. It's written on the department account, not from the director himself."

Something sounded funny. "Wait. The director is still with us... right?"

She turned toward the coffee maker before I could see her expression. "Actually, as I understand things, Frank and his frail wife are packing up their belongings as we speak."

"He's leaving, too?" This was one of my nightmares about departing the security of the States and coming to a foreign country where nearly everything operated by such irregular and fragile standards. "So now they'll have another lengthy talent search and it'll slow down all the reforms you and the team has worked on."

"Not necessarily."

"Which part?"

"No time now, Larry. You need to get dressed." It was only then that I fully realized Yvonne was already attired as though she were immediately headed to her department. "We're expected in the new president's office in twenty minutes."

"I can't be ready in twenty minutes. I just got up. Haven't eaten anything. I'm not even awake yet."

"Make an effort, dear. This is probably your first visit with our new president and first impressions count."

It would certainly be our first meeting. "Does he speak English?"

"Perfectly."

"Had you met him before?"

"I've tutored his children, dear. Don't you remember?"

We'd only been there eight months and she'd been working eleven-hour days. "When did you have time to tutor anybody?"

"Better hurry, Larry. We don't want to keep His Excellency waiting."

THOUGH WE'D ARRIVED on time, we were naturally forced to wait. It was a tactic used throughout administrative offices in America, and likely everywhere else. *Make 'em sweat.* However, it seemed I was the only one sweating—Yvonne looked fresh as a daisy. She'd always been better in crises.

Finally, about half an hour after our appointment time, a nervous-looking functionary ushered us in and announced us as Yvonne Carter and husband.

After a hesitation that could have been absent-mindedness or possibly mere theatrics, President Ortiz waved us toward two upholstered chairs in front of his massive wooden desk. There was no apology in his explanation: "So many adjustments when the upper levels of government are realigned."

As Ortiz strolled about his new office, seeming to notice something different with each circuit, we both remained silent. Finally he took his own seat, leaned back, and eyed us carefully—first Yvonne... then me... then her again. "I've been briefed on the educational reforms," he said, without revealing if that was a good thing or bad. "Fundamentally a solid approach to our problems of literacy and learning, but parts of the history section will need to be, shall we say, revised." After a thin smile, he added, "Recent history... the governmental reorganization."

"Yes, Your Excellency," replied Yvonne. "In fact, anticipating your likely desires in that regard, I've already been working on the changes this very morning. I'll have the drafts by tomorrow and we can have them fully integrated within the first week."

I knew Yvonne had been up long before I rose that morning, but I was astonished that she'd already been working on a historical account of the coup… or whatever they might call it when Ortiz's censors got through with it.

"Exactly as I'd hoped," he said, looking her in the eyes. "I feel quite confident that my administration will be a beneficent friend of the new Education Department." Suddenly he stood again, made another circuit around the entire office, and stood military-straight behind his own chair. Then, eyeing me, he repeated one of his first themes of our session, "So many adjustments during realignments…"

"Excellency, you can be certain of the full support of the Education Department and all its staff," added Yvonne, rather solicitously.

Ortiz just nodded. There was more back and forth chitchat—between him and her—which seemed to imply something completely different than the literal meaning of its words. His words also hinted of menace and I sensed His Excellency was toying with me for some reason. Couldn't quite put my finger on it, but it felt like he was somehow testing me… as though wondering if I had the *right stuff.*

Yvonne had become strangely quiet. It was difficult to tell whether she just possessed more steel in her backbone or whether this interview was more comfortable for her because she'd been around Ortiz—on whichever occasions when she'd privately tutored his young children. Of course, that had been before he was elevated to the supreme ruler of that region.

Back then, Ortiz had been merely a rising colonel, young for that rank, but powerful with many friends. Out of the blue, I'd learned on our hurried walk over to his palace, most of the generals had either fled the country, been placed under house arrest, or simply disappeared. And Col. Ortiz leaped over the more senior colonels to become their leader. I had to assume he'd consolidated the strong backing of many in the military, as well as key players like the head of the internal state security service.

Some of what Ortiz said was somehow tuned out by my apprehensive brain—it seemed adrenaline was partly shutting down my comprehension. By the time I'd tuned back in, he seemed to be concluding. "I'm glad we had this opportunity to clarify any uncertainties about the leadership of our Education Department." It almost sounded like we'd just received our pink slips.

Yvonne nodded, but remained silent.

"I'm not sure I understand, Your Excellency, about our contracts... our placements," I said tentatively. "Where do you need our services in your new government?"

"Precisely the point I was getting to," he replied calmly, as he pressed a silent button on a small console at the right of his tidy desktop.

I'd already heard rumors of what that button meant when used by the former president, but there are buttons and then there are *buttons*. Surely the signal for the new Minister of Education would be on the same console as the buzzer for the chief bureaucrats for finance, public works, foreign affairs, et cetera... as well as his head advisors in the police, the military, and the dreaded, powerful internal state security service. I found myself trembling as I waited to see who would enter the office door.

Glancing over at Yvonne, with the intent of reassuring her, I noted she continued to appear remarkably calm.

A discreet knock at the reinforced door caused all of us to turn that way. Before His Excellency responded to whoever was behind that door, he looked at me with an expression of complete indifference... as if my chair were empty. But to Yvonne, he smiled warmly.

No reply from her besides another brief nod.

Then His Excellency turned back to me, saying, "And that point I was about to make, Mr. Carter, is simply that I do not require the services of Mr. and Mrs. Carter."

"You mean we both have to leave? But our contract..."

"Never mind any contracts my predecessor found amusing. I've reassessed everything in this government and it's time to trim away some of the waste... those redundant services, no longer needed nor desired."

"How long do we have to pack up?"

"Very little packing will be necessary, Mr. Carter. While we've been discussing these matters, my prior arrangements have already relocated what is necessary to the new quarters."

"But I need to be present when they pack my books and papers. Everything's in a very specific order. My project... that is, the research I was working on under that grant..."

He waved his newly majestic hand. "Your books and papers received the care to which they were entitled."

I breathed out a sigh—but not of relief—more related to nerves and tension. "Begging your pardon, Excellency, but I'm still unclear how much time before we begin our new duties."

He looked vaguely surprised and then stole a quick glance at Yvonne. "Oh, do you not yet comprehend, Mr. Carter?"

Looking first at Yvonne, where I detected nothing, then at our new ruler, I replied, rather shakily, "No, Excellency, I'm afraid I'm still in the dark."

"Indeed... indeed. In the dark. Quite apropos, Mr. Carter." Then he turned again to the door, where the individual he'd previously buzzed still awaited permission to enter. "Come," he said, simply and loudly enough to be heard through the thick door. Then, to me, he added, "You see, Mr. Carter, what I've been explaining is that your services are no longer required."

"But we..."

"You're not listening, I'm afraid." Then he pointed a blunt, thick finger directly at my forehead. "*Your* services are not required. However, I have made arrangements for your talented and lovely ex-wife."

"But we're still married."

"Only for a few more seconds, Mr. Carter. I have the full authority of the state to perform ceremonies, including marriages. Therefore, obviously, the unhindered power to dissolve those unions." And he waved in the man standing in the doorway—Raphael, the chief of the internal state security service, wearing plain clothes, an ill-fitting suit. Behind him were two tall, impassive officers in crisp black uniforms. "You'll have just enough time to tell your wife good-bye, Mr. Carter."

With desperation and more terror than I thought my system could withstand, I looked again at Yvonne... and was shocked to see a pleasant smile—the coolish one she used at parties—on her face. Then she said, simply, "I'll be with you momentarily, Excellency."

END

The Room

Charles A. Salter

BRYCE ONLY HAD TWO. Just two glasses at the Four Oaks Country Club Champagne Brunch in Orlando. He knew he could pass the breathalyzer test but that he would probably go to jail anyway. Not fair. Not right.

She had been guzzling like an alkie all morning—at least eight before he'd lost count—yet she would likely get off scot-free. Not fair, and Bryce always liked to make things more fair... for him.

Always.

He turned to her in the front passenger seat of his half-mil flame red Maserati, the paint's color obscuring the human blood on the front fender. She had the same silly grin she'd had earlier at the table when he'd made his move to get her out of there, back to his place. But now she was humming that bloody awful "Sweet Dreams are Made of This" by the Eurythmics and twirling her long blonde locks with her fingers, the nails garishly painted purple. Just moments before, he'd had one hand tangling with her La Perla Modernista bra, the other hand fumbling to get beneath her matching black panties. Now her plump flesh disgusted him. She had the money but lacked the class of the sorority girls back on campus.

As she turned towards him and spoke, the smell out of her mouth of salty Beluga caviar, garlic toast tips, and the golden Moet nauseated him. He couldn't even remember her name.

"Who was driving?" he demanded.

"You're stupider than you look. No one was driving."

"Listen, bitch, if we both expect to survive this, we've got to get our story straight."

She rolled her eyes and looked out the passenger window at the pedestrian's flecks of blood on the glass. "No one was driving. That's the truth, and the truth is easier to remember when they cross-exam you for hours. I've been through this before, you know. I can handle the cops. Just smile at special moments, show a little skin, twirl my hair, and tell the truth. Never fails."

"This time the truth will get us nailed and we'll both go to jail. I know I can pass the BAC—I only had two Moets, and ate lots of eggs benedict. Now, who was driving?"

"You? You were driving?" she asked with uncertainty.

He reached over and pulled the strands of hair out of her fingers, purposely tugging on the scalp hard 'til she yelped. "You can't question it. You have to sound sure of yourself. Who was driving?"

She gasped and rubbed her head. "*You* were driving."

"I was driving. You can never change that story. You can never say anything else to anyone. Who was driving? Bryce Carlton was driving." He gave another sharp tug on her hair. "Got it?"

"Stop that, you little shit," she gasped. "You're hurting me. I got it. Bryce Carlton was driving."

He let go of her hair. "How did we meet?"

"You know how. You got to the brunch and saw me with a crowd of friends and weaseled your way into our group."

"That's good. That's the truth. We've got to have a layer of truth in this, and every one who saw us at Four Oaks can back that up. We just randomly met. Don't say weasel, though. Make up some shit about people liking my Brooks Brothers suit, or my athletic form, or college good looks. Something positive."

She snickered. "Yeah, officer, I got one look at his broad shoulders, muscular chest, and slim waist and just melted, so I waved him over."

Bryce smiled for the first time. "That's good. That sounds real enough. You had the hots for me, and after one look at you, I didn't see anyone else in the room all morning. Stick with that."

"Whatever you say. Just quit hurting me. Geez, I thought I liked you."

"Why did you take me to the Appian Way, tell me to quit driving, scoot over, have sex, and let the car roll down the hill by itself?"

She laughed. "Because my father helped design this road. It's the first road in Florida so well-engineered that a car can careen down it unguided and not sail off the pavement and hit the shoulder ridges, trees, signs, or anything. Very sexy. You wouldn't believe the thrill of your Big O while doing it in a car tuffin' down the road on its own."

"You took me to see the handiwork of your father, the highway engineer. But I never stopped driving and never left the wheel with the car in motion. You got that?"

She pulled her head back so he couldn't grab her hair again. "Yeah, you were driving the whole time. Bryce Carlton was driving."

"And who is that kid we just hit? The one who had been drinking with us and then followed us out here."

"That was my lover."

"Your *lover?* Then why are you resting here inside the car while he's bleeding out there?"

"I didn't say I liked him. Not any more. He's way too jealous... thinks he owns me... serves him right anyway, getting out of his car and running around in front of us like an idiot."

Her lover is the victim. Her father is a local VIP. I'm the outsider from Yankee-land. I need more insurance. "Our only mistake was not putting seat belts on." Bryce resumed his position at the wheel, took a sharp breath, then shot his head forward in a fierce karate strike, banging his forehead into the wheel. He came back up, eyes watering, with a red bruise blooming on his skin.

"Geez! What the hell did you do that for? Are you crazy?"

"Just in case there is a question about why we are woozy and the details of our stories might be a little fuzzy. We're not drunk. We got injured in the collision."

"I didn't get injured. I'm just drunk as a Florida skunk."

He suddenly bolted towards her, grabbed both her shoulders, and flung her head-first into the dashboard with all the force he could muster.

There was a mushy crunching sound, but she didn't vocalize. He pulled her up and let her lie limply back in the seat. She was out cold, but still breathing.

Then the siren got closer and the swirling colored lights fell upon them.

❧

The Room, Day 1

BRYCE SAT AT A plain wooden table bolted to the floor. He saw nothing else in the room but a spare chair, a one-way mirror facing him, and two surveillance cameras, one in each ceiling corner above the mirror.

Without so much as a knock, the door opened and in shuffled a long-haired fellow with a scruffy beard and a worn grey suit with no tie.

Bryce thought he looked like half the male professors he had seen back at college in Boston.

The man paced back and forth, all over the room, forcing Bryce to follow constantly with his eyes, while the man himself made no eye contact and seemed pre-occupied.

Finally he spoke. "Bryce Carlton, right? I'm in the right room?"

Bryce nodded silently.

"I'm Dr. Alt, your court-appointed forensic psychiatrist. We're going to be in this room together for exactly one hour each day for three days in a row. When that clock on the wall behind you reaches ten hundred hours each day, we will start. When it reaches eleven hundred hours, we will stop. Clear?"

Bryce nodded again.

"The most important thing for you to understand is that you can speak freely with me in this room during these sessions. Nothing you say in this room and during that time can be used against you in a court of law, not unless you also repeat it outside of this room and timeframe. Clear?"

Again a nod.

Alt abruptly scraped the empty chair across the tiled floor and sat down at the table opposite him, at last casting a fierce, searching gaze into Bryce's face. "I'm here to determine if you are insane enough to withstand a trial for these alleged crimes."

Bryce protested. "*In*sane? Don't you mean *sane*?"

Alt's dark eyes penetrated deeply into Bryce's soul. "You just failed the first test. You are perfectly capable of understanding and using language and immediately noting a logical contradiction."

Bryce sputtered, "There's no point in me talking to you at all if everything I say is taken to support your pre-ordained conclusion!"

"You just failed the second test. You are able to apprehend your own actions, how they might influence your future, and thus inhibit your responses so as to minimize the risk to yourself."

Bryce mumbled a curse word beneath his breath.

"I find you completely and thoroughly sane and ready to stand trial. I could write my report immediately and spare us the need for three complete sessions. Convince me I'm wrong."

Bryce grew red in the face and started to speak, then checked himself. He glared right back into the eyes of Dr. Alt without blinking, trying to outstare him.

Dr. Alt broke away first, slid back his chair, stood up and began to pace again, humming something to himself.

Bryce knew a little about classical music, but couldn't pin this one down. Yet it sounded awfully familiar, like something dramatic from an old European symphony or opera he had heard before. Wagner, maybe?

The minutes passed with neither man speaking. It seemed like over an hour to Bryce. Surely it had to be almost 11:00 AM!

Bryce imagined the clock behind him ticking audibly. He turned to see it for the first time, wondering why he hadn't noted it when the guard initially brought him in. Only 10:16.

To kill time, Bryce spoke. "So you're a shrink, huh?"

Dr. Alt stopped pacing and stared at Bryce from the other side of the room. "That's the most ludicrous word in the entire history of medicine. How does coming to understand someone's mind shrink it? I'm a *psychiatrist*."

Bryce could feel his armpits growing moister. He tried again. "So you're a Freudian, eh?"

"As far as I'm concerned, Sigmund Freud was a giant doofus. To the extent his insights and writings had any validity at all, it was only during the height of the Victorian period, from the late 19th century through the early decades of the 20th. A time when all sexual impulses were dramatically repressed by society. In case you hadn't noticed, all that changed completely in the 1960s."

Dr. Alt returned to his seat, visually scouring Bryce's face for something... maybe anything. "That's the way it goes with cultural cycles; every couple of generations the pendulum swings way out to the farthest right wing, only to provoke a massive cultural reaction. Then over a few decades, it swings back in the other direction, to the farthest left wing for a while."

Bryce looked away.

"Now we're overdue to swing back towards something resembling normal humanity for its turn. But not you. Too bad for you. You are stuck on that most extreme end of unlimited impulse gratification, aren't you? That's what led to your crimes this past weekend, right?"

Alt went silent and just stared at Bryce.

The latter broke his gaze from Alt and then looked down and around the room. He began to fidget as the silence grew, minute by minute. Finally Bryce said, "What are you doing? What are you waiting for? Why are you wasting my time with these long silences?"

"I'm waiting to see if you will ask about the welfare of the young lady, your date for the weekend, who was in the car with you and smashed her head into the dash when you collided with that pedestrian."

"I thought you were asking the questions. I didn't think it was polite for me to question you."

More uncomfortable silence, as Bryce grew more agitated. "All right! All right! How is she?"

"How is who?"

Carlton raised his fist and then pounded the table once. "You know, the girl in the car!"

"What is her name?"

"I don't... Courtney, Carol, Columbia... something with a C. Oh, I know, Christina. How is Christina?"

"She's in a coma. How much did you have to drink at the brunch yesterday, Mr. Carlton?"

"I only had two glasses of champagne."

"Yes, we know. Way less than everyone else at the table. Were you trawling for tail that morning? Picking up girls you barely knew the name of for carnal encounters? You wanted them drunk, but you planned to stay sober, making it easier for you to dominate them."

"My sexual proclivities are solely my own business."

"Not entirely, not in a case like this. That half-million dollar Maserati wasn't even yours, was it? You spent a fortune renting the flashiest babe magnet you could find, didn't you? Do you feel so insecure in your masculinity that you need to show off at great expense to attract easy lays who would shed their drawers just as readily for a cool guy in a decent Ford or Chevy?"

"Why are you talking about her like that? She's a nice country club girl from a good family."

"Irrelevant." Alt looked away, then back. "Red car, red the color of blood," then he went silent and stared at the college boy.

Bryce stared back, staring without blinking, accepting the shrink's challenge and throwing down the gauntlet. Finally he blinked and said, "All right, all right, how is the pedestrian we hit?"

"Dead."

"Dead? We barely bumped him. He fell and I saw his shirt turning red in a little patch on the lower left back, but then he jumped up, laughed, and said 'I'm okay!'"

"Luckily for you, nothing you say in this interview in this office can be used against you in a court of law."

"What do you mean? What did I say?"

"You just confessed to hitting a pedestrian. Mr. Carlton, were you two doing the Ape Slide that evening?"

"I've never even heard the term."

"But you know what I mean, don't you? Thrill seekers love to drive to the top of that low hill and do their thing as the car glides down on its own. Didn't you notice the sign at the top of the hill stating that it was unlawful to attempt that and that even if no incident occurs you can go to jail for reckless endangerment?"

"I never noticed a sign like that and, in any event, was in full control of the vehicle at all times. That fellow was at fault, jumping in front of us like that. I braked immediately, but the car couldn't stop fast enough to avoid hitting him."

"Why do you say that fellow, like you didn't know him? He was eating and drinking with you all at your brunch table the entire morning."

"Yeah, but I never caught his name. We didn't talk directly or get introduced or anything. There were three or four people seated between us."

"Did you catch any of their names?"

"No."

"You're not very good with names, are you?"

"I got your name okay. You're Dr. Alt. So who was the guy that got hurt?"

"You mean *killed*, not hurt. It was Gerald Appius, the brother of your date, Christina Appius."

Bryce felt queasy. *So they were sibs as well as lovers. And this guy already knows everything, so why are we here?* "Her father designed the Appian Way, she said. She was proud of him and the first perfectly safe road in America and wanted to show me. I told you it was a nice family. So terrible to have two misfortunes in one day in one nice family."

"You say misfortune as if it were an act of nature. It was an act by you! *Your* act! Tell me about *your* family."

"Not much to tell. I'm an only child."

"Really?" Dr. Alt glanced up at the clock. "Time's up. Eleven hundred hours. We'll resume tomorrow." And with that, Dr. Alt shuffled from the room.

Bryce slowly let out a deep breath.

⌒⁄⌒

The Room, Day 2

AS HE SAT IN the room waiting for the clock to reach 10:00 AM, Bryce noted a faint sound of music being piped in. He recognized it immediately as the same melody Dr. Alt had been humming the day before. *How odd. Did Alt hear this yesterday and spontaneously pick it up or did he plan this music and arrange for them to play it? What does it* mean?

The ticking of the clock behind him seemed louder and louder. He glanced back. 9:59 AM. He waited and waited as long as he could stand it. Then he started reliving his dream of last night, one in which he saw the recent auto accident from the point of view of the man who'd been killed, Gerald Appius. Bryce imagined he saw the blood red Maserati plowing towards and into him, as he helplessly looked through the windshield to see the driver ignoring the road and molesting his sister. As Gerald, he saw and shouted "Stop!" and then felt the massive object crush into his body like a battering ram.

Finally the door opened and Dr. Alt entered.

Bryce was ready to call the man out for being late, but as he began to speak he glanced back at the clock and it read 10:00.

56

Alt cleared his throat. "Before we proceed, I need to remind you that everything you say in this room to me during this hour is confidential. Nothing you say in this room to me can be used against you in a court of law, unless—" and here the man paused for emphasis "—you yourself repeat it outside of this room and this timeframe. Clear?"

Bryce nodded. "So you still aren't sure whether I'm a nut after all?"

"That term is meaningless to me. I have to determine whether you are legally insane and assure the court about the state of your ability to make judgments on your own behalf."

"So now you're questioning not just my sanity but my judgment?"

"Mr. Carlton, you obviously are a young man of some intelligence, education, and worldly experience. Yet when the arresting officer read you your rights at the scene of the incident, you waived them and began to describe your version of what happened. And at the station later, you declined to use your phone call to rally a lawyer, family member, or friend to your side."

"I've got nothing to hide. I'm completely innocent and cooperating with the police in every way."

"So you say, but I think not. In any event, you've also sustained a blow to the head which may be affecting your mental abilities, and my job is to determine whether we need to bring this before the court to determine whether you should be placed under psychiatric custody until they can determine if you are competent to continue with the case."

"So now you're not sure I'm competent."

"I believe you are sane, competent, capable of sound judgment... and... completely guilty. But my personal beliefs are irrelevant—it's what I can prove to the court which counts."

Bryce whined, "You said what happened in this room cannot be used in court."

"Not used *against* you. It can be used to exonerate you. You know what I really think, Mr. Carlton?"

The young man shrugged.

"I think your conscience is eating away at you."

"Conscience? You believe in fairy tales?"

"No, Mr. Carlton, not fairy tales. You are not a psychopath, devoid of conscience. You just have yours buried pretty deep. But beware... if the police can't find you out, your own conscience may finally emerge and give you away. It takes a lot of energy to keep that thing buried. Most men can't keep it suppressed forever."

"I'm tired of your philosophizing."

Alt shrugged.

"How did you get a name like Alt anyway? That's German for *old*, isn't it? You're Dr. Old."

"Insulting me doesn't get you anywhere. If the name bothers you, just think of me as your alter ego."

"Are you for real?"

"I'm as real as you are. Would you like some coffee or water before we really get down to business today?"

Bryce shook his head.

"So, you told the arresting officer you were down in Orlando for spring break. You're from Harvard."

The young man nodded.

"How do you like Boston?"

"I said Harvard. That's Cambridge, not Boston."

"The main campus is in Cambridge, but the Harvard Medical School and Harvard School of Public Health are in Boston. That's where I went to school. You flew in from Boston, I understand. It's just across the Charles River from Cambridge, so why are you obfuscating? They're both parts of one continuous urban area."

"I'm not obfuscating. I'm being precise."

"What's the name of your library?"

"The Widener Library."

"What does Memorial Hall commemorate?"

"Harvard's Civil War dead."

"What's the name of that prized coffee shop in Harvard Square?"

"What the hell is this?" Bryce's cheeks turned pink. "You're acting like you don't believe I'm really from Harvard. It's easy enough to prove. Look at the ID in my wallet. Check with the landlady where I live."

"We did all that. I don't doubt you're from Harvard. I'm checking for memory loss, mental confusion, aphasias, things caused by the blow to your head that might affect your ability to make sound decisions on your own behalf in court."

Bryce shrugged in frustration, grunted, and shook his head.

"What is the name of the Harvard University Library?"

"The Widener Library."

"Is MIT on the Cambridge side of the river or the Boston side?"

"On the Cambridge side, about midway between the two Harvard campuses."

"Why did you remove yourself from the controls of a moving car that evening and scoot towards the girl in the other seat? Were you all hot and horny and trying to get it on as the uncontrolled car glided down? Eager to do the Ape Slide for kicks?"

"I didn't let go. I was in control of the vehicle at all times. I'm sure Christina can verify that I was driving."

"Maybe... if she comes out of the coma. Tell me about your family."

"There's not much to tell. I'd rather not get into it."

"What's the name of the main Harvard University Library?"

"I already told you ten times. The Widener Library."

"What's the name of the library where you worked?"

"I'm getting fed up with this! The Widener Library."

"What's the name of the library where you live?"

"The—" He froze in mid-phrase, his mouth open. "—the Harvard Public Library."

Dr. Alt smiled. "Now we're getting somewhere. You're not a preppy with a rich daddy who owns Maseratis and a fancy vacation home on Martha's Vineyard. You're not really from Harvard University. You're a fraud, a poseur. You'd never be able to pass yourself off as a wealthy Harvard kid in Boston, where people know you. So you decided to fly down to Florida for spring break and mix it up with local young lovelies who would see your expensive Maserati and believe anything you told them."

Bryce began to tremble.

"But you're not wealthy at all. You live in a rural town also called, by sheer coincidence, Harvard, some twenty-five miles northwest of Boston, thirty or more miles from the Cambridge main campus of the like-named university. Your only connection with the university is when you worked at the Widener Library one summer checking out books and re-shelving returns. That doesn't pay enough for you to fly down here and rent a Maserati, so where did you get the money?"

Bryce was visibly shaking now, but refused to open his mouth. He slumped in the chair, crossed his arms across his chest in a classic self-protective pose, and tilted his head down, glaring angrily at the floor.

"Where did you get the money, Carlton? Where?"

Alt looked at the clock. "Time's up for today, Bryce Carlton. But we'll pick this up tomorrow. You might have fooled the local young lovelies... you might have fooled even the arresting police officer, but you haven't fooled me. You can never fool me. I am the voice of your conscience and I can see right through you!"

∽

The Room, Day 3

AS HE WAITED FOR Dr. Alt to appear, Bryce recognized the same music as previous days coming into the room, and growing louder and louder.

He imagined the clock behind him had a louder click precisely at 10:00 AM, just as Alt entered the room.

The psychiatrist spoke first. "Let me remind you about the rules for our time in this—"

Bryce angrily waved his hands. "Enough already, I remember the rules."

"Are you in a better mood than yesterday? You got quite angry with me yesterday, and I am only here to help you find the truth."

"My moods have nothing to do with anything and are none of your business."

"Maybe... maybe not." Alt had been pacing as usual, but then drew up his chair with a scratching screech along the floor and sat down facing the younger man. "You so far have avoided discussing anything about your own family, so today we are going to get into that."

"Maybe you will; I'm not talking about them."

"Talk or not... I can read your mind. I will tell *you* about them."

Bryce wrapped his arms around himself and looked at the floor.

"You never knew your father. You were raised by a single mother who never told you a thing about him. By the time you were eight years old, you stopped asking."

"You're making me angry again," Bryce spouted. "How could a man I never knew have anything to do with what's happening now?"

"One day you finally found an old letter in your mother's secret hiding place. Dated the year before you were born. It held a postmark... from Orlando, Florida."

"You're a frickin' liar!"

"*That's* why you chose Florida for spring break. It wasn't just the pretty girls and the chances for easy sex in the jazzed-up party scene that you wanted. Most college kids on spring break head to the Florida beaches like Daytona, South Beach, or Panama City Beach. But you chose an inland city like Orlando, where the spring break action is way more limited. You wanted to find some connection with your father, however tenuous or remote. Something that might help you understand him... his motivations... why he may have impregnated your mother and then abandoned you both."

"That's just more BS speculation that has nothing to do with what happened this week."

"She's dead, you know," said Alt.

"Who's dead?"

"Christina Appius, your 'date' for spring break. She died this morning, about ninety minutes ago."

Bryce took his first easy breath of the morning. "So she never came out of her coma?"

"Correct. Luckily for you, she never had the chance to tell the truth about that day, the Appian Way, and how you killed her and her brother."

"I never killed anyone!" Bryce spat back, sending visible flecks of saliva into the air.

Alt sat further back in his seat. "Oh, I grant you it wasn't pre-meditated, first degree murder. You won't get The Chair. Not for that, anyway."

"The Chair? You are so full of crap. No one gets that these days. It's lethal injection."

"Figure of speech," said Alt, standing up and resuming his pacing. The same music as before got louder and louder. "But you obviously do know about capital crimes and capital punishment, so you are fully capable of apprehending possible consequences for your criminal actions. No, not first degree murder this week in Orlando, just reckless endangerment, involuntary manslaughter for both brother and sister, assault and battery on the girl. Yes, we know you threw her head into the dash—no collision at that slow speed with a pedestrian could possibly have caused such a forceful dislocation within the vehicle, one which fractured two vertebrae in her neck. You probably hit your own head purposefully as well, though you were careful to use a lot less force when banging yourself up than when banging her."

Bryce was speechless.

"You'll probably get no more than twenty years in a Florida state pen for all that. I mean, I'm not your lawyer, DA, jury, or judge, but I've been around the courts long enough to have a good idea of what you're liable to get... for *that*."

Bryce felt his temper welling up within him and was getting fed up with Alt and that terrible symphonic music. "Why are you piping more and more of that awful music in here for each session?"

"To get you in the proper frame of mind to confront honestly your issues."

"What is that music, anyway?"

Dr. Alt hummed a few bars along with the input entering the room. "It's by the 19th century French composer Hector Berlioz. In French the opera was originally called *La Damnation de Faust*. Are you familiar with the Faust story, either from that opera or the prior epic by Goethe, or any of the countless other versions?"

"Yeah, vaguely. I saw the Goethe version in the Widener once and skimmed a bit before reshelving it."

"It's quite the story, Mr. Carlton. Faust lusts after a young beauty named Marguerite and with the help of Mephistopheles seduces but then abandons her. In the Berlioz version, Faust later learns that Marguerite has accidentally killed her own mother and is due to hang. Mephistopheles offers to help Faust save her... at the cost of his own soul. But as Mephistopheles leads Faust forward, the condemned man gradually realizes he is being led not to Marguerite to help her... but... into hell. Very powerful music in that part. We're about to get there now."

"Turn it off!" yelled Bryce.

"No! Let it play while we get back to your family. Why did you kill her, Mr. Carlton? Was it just for the money or did you become enraged because she had withheld from you the truth about your father?"

"Turn it off!" screamed Bryce, rising to his feet and gripping the chair's back firmly.

"No! We're almost at the end, where Faust begins to recognize the demons surrounding him. I'll have them turn the music off when it ends. Now tell me the truth, Mr. Carlton. Why did you kill her and leave her in the closet, where the police will find her in a couple of days, when the smell gets strong enough to scare the landlady?"

"This is the last time I'm going to tell you! Turn off that damnable music or I'm going to bash your head in with this chair!"

Dr. Alt wouldn't yield. "If you went there intending to kill her, that's murder one. Even in liberal Massachusetts, you're liable to get life for that. Or did you initially just plan to ask for money and information on how you could find your father, but then things got out of control when she refused to help? You might get murder in the second degree for that. But you'll never be able to plea it down below that, not without a full and honest confession. Not after hiding the body, refusing to report the incident, and fleeing across state lines. No DA in his right mind will now accept a plea less than second degree."

Bryce roared like a trapped lion. Muscles bulging, he lifted the chair overhead and rushed Dr. Alt, crashing the chair into his head and shoulders again and again, smashing his face.

The chair splintered, and sharp spikes of wood penetrated his own face, too.

Blood spattered everywhere. Blood on his own lips, too. He no longer knew for sure which might be his blood and which was the blood of his nemesis.

Dr. Alt lay crumpled and wet with red on the floor. Silent at last. Finally silent.

Bryce dropped the remains of the chair legs in his hand, flung open the door of the interrogation room, and ran out screaming. "I confess! I did it! I killed them all! My mother, the Appius twins, Dr. Alt—all of them!"

He collapsed to the PD station floor as detectives surrounded him and took him back into custody.

⚮

THE PUBLIC DEFENDER assigned to Bryce Carlton angrily demanded to see the detective in charge of the case, then poured out the tale he had just heard of a sadistic psychiatrist named Dr. Alt who mentally badgered and physically beat the young man into making a false confession. "And he has the wounds to prove it," concluded lawyer Ed Perkins. "I saw them myself."

"Those were self-inflicted," said Detective Sergeant Lucent. "We have him on videotape from two different angles whacking himself all over with a chair. No one here laid a hand on him."

"Well, what about all that verbal abuse, accusations, and badgering until my client was an emotional wreck and confessed just to end it all? What about that room he calls the punishment room?"

"Oh, that!" exclaimed Lucent. "We call that the conscience room. We simply leave a suspect in there for an hour or so each day, to sit totally alone with his thoughts. Guilty ones start to imagine things and even develop elaborate fantasy interactions sometimes. They dwell more and more on their guilt and often confess without us so much as having to ask a single question."

"That's unbelievable. That won't hold up in court. I'm going to not only get him off on all counts, but we are going to sue the entire police department and city 'til this boy is set for life."

"Why should it not hold up in court? We can show you three hours of tape from each camera, proving he was in the room completely alone every minute. Sometimes he would sit quietly, other times he would argue with himself, bang the table, leap up in anger and shuffle about the room like a caged animal. In the third hour, he got visibly agitated and began beating himself with a chair and screaming at some being or beings who weren't even there. Then he emerged in a panic screaming out his full confession."

"What about that sadistic music that unnerved him so? Are you running an Abu Ghraib here? This violates his constitutional rights."

"Sadistic music?" laughed Lucent. "We have a library of classical music and pipe that in to give people something to focus on when they are alone, to occupy their minds. Any music instructor at any educational institution in this country could testify in court to the calming and other beneficial effects of good classical music. You can hear it for yourself on our recorded videos of Carlton in the conscience room. Music lovers the world over pay good money to hear that kind of quality music at concerts and via recordings of same."

Perkins looked stunned, all his aspirations for easy courtroom victory seemingly dashed.

"Look, Mr. Perkins. I know you are brand new to the public defenders' office and not yet familiar with how we do things down here. I'm not going to tell you how to handle your case, but it seems pretty obvious to me. I mean, there is video of him talking to beings who aren't even there, of your client confessing to murdering someone who doesn't even exist, this Dr. Alt character he invented. Isn't your plea rather obvious?"

The light in Perkins' head seemed to click, but he still looked dubious. "But Bryce Carlton said that music was *evil*, designed to torment him and make him confess. It also made him confess to three deaths that are real..."

Detective Sergeant Lucent smiled, maybe just a bit too much. "*Evil* music? First time I've heard that one. Good classical music helps to focus the mind on the deeper, ultimate realities in life, on what's really important... does it really matter if in this case it made Carlton project an imaginary image of his real Harvard Medical School father into the room with him? The long-haired, scraggly-bearded Dr. Josef Schildkraut Alt, graduate of Harvard Med, who impregnated one Amanda Carlton during spring break on Martha's Vineyard and died in a tragic car accident on the Massachusetts Turnpike exactly one year after his bastard progeny was born? Where's the harm in him finally meeting his own true father, even if only in his imagination?"

END

Murder on Her Mind

J. L. Salter

October 15—Monday—early morning
"AND YOU THINK IT'S normal for a hubby to play nice?" My earnest but often fanatical friend Holly Salles was on another tear. "How naïve can you be, Janet?"

"What are you on about now?" I asked, though I'd already guessed. Recently, it was a frequent topic of hers, since she was currently so engrossed in numerous TV shows focusing on suspicious deaths, often by spouses. After brewing this pot of tea, my husband had just left for his loan officer job at the bank—and immediately Holly had zoomed here from across the street. *She must have been watching out her window.* "I think it's somewhat endearing that Bill is being more attentive," I replied as I clutched my second mug of green tea for the morning.

"Attentive?" replied Holly in a voice so high it squeaked. "Serving you hot beverages all of a sudden is totally abnormal. He's got to have an angle." She leaned very close to my mug and—with her fingers—waved toward herself a bit of its aroma. "Yikes. What is that?"

"I told you when you walked in." I took another sip. True, it was a bit harsh compared to my usual brand, but people in Ceylon or wherever have different taste buds. "You want to try some?"

"Absolutely not!" she said, jerking her head backwards like she'd heard a rattlesnake. "You know we don't do tea or coffee at my house. We're all about organic vitamins and supplements."

Since she didn't mention the cleanses she'd tried to get me to try, I didn't bring them up.

"You know," she continued. "Healthy stuff."

Thus far I had not mentioned this to Holly, but she had been looking less and less healthy since she and Darren had begun taking all those pricey organic herbs and exotic mixtures. I had no way to measure the actual pounds involved, but it was easy to see she had dropped too many... and too fast. "Maybe you should slow down on all that healthy stuff and just eat some pizza or cheeseburgers once in a while."

"I know what you're doing," she said, and then jutted her jaw. "You're deflecting the real subject here and trying to get me all..."

"So what is the real subject, Holly?"

After motioning for me to put down my mug, my friend reached for both my hands and held them tenderly. For a long moment, she stared into my eyes. "I'm trying to keep you from becoming a statistic, Janet. Just the other night I watched a show and you wouldn't believe how prevalent *wife-a-cide* is in these times."

She'd mentioned this before but never yet remembered the correct term, *uxoricide*. Which was understandable, since I'd had to look it up.

"Look, Holly, you're making a big deal out of nothing. I don't know very much about tea, other than what I consider the standard British blends. As far as I'm concerned, a Lapsang Souchong could be a rich man's Shitzsu. All I'm saying is that I think it's kind of sweet that my husband's suddenly making tea for me most mornings before he goes to work."

"I've been telling you..." she trailed off, apparently incredulous that I could be so naïve as to accept a simple act of husbandly kindness at face value.

To this point in our friendship, when Holly had been on a tear about someone we both knew—or someone I'd never heard of, for that matter—I'd just listened as politely as I could manage until I was able to ease her over to a different subject. All that fascination with death and murder seemed distinctly unhealthy to me and I was certain she was addicted to the adrenaline of capital crime investigation and cold case forensics. *At least the way those are presented on television.*

"Show me this lappy souchy stuff he's been plying you with," she said, horribly butchering the actual name.

"If you're so interested, go look in my pantry and see for yourself." I had no intention of encouraging her morbid curiosity. "I'm not getting up. My tummy has a bit of flutter."

"That's one of the signs," she said, over her shoulder, as she headed toward my kitchen.

I've found that people who drink supplements that look like dirty dishwater—and taste no better—have a missionary zeal to criticize the diets of others. Their prevailing credo seems to be, *If I'm drinking seaweed extract... everyone should have to.*

When she reached my pantry, Holly quickly dropped her previous thread. "Don't you shop any more, Janet?"

"Sure I do. Every Sunday afternoon. You know that."

"No way... unless you've been donating it all to a shelter somewhere."

I'd been a bit off my game lately in the concentration department and Holly's interrogation was throwing me. "What do you mean?"

"There's not enough food in here to feed a church rodent."

Grimacing slightly, I stood and declared defiantly, "You're subsisting on herbs and organic cleanses and you're lecturing *me* about groceries?"

"Never mind. It's not the food I'm concerned with anyhow. It's all these exotic tea blends." She pulled out two small tins. "This is what I'm talking about. Never, never drink a tea that didn't come already bagged and sealed in a foil pouch. These little cans have the shriveled tea leaves all loosey goosey and anybody could put anything in there."

"Do you see anything in there besides tea leaves?"

"I wouldn't know a tea leaf from a hemlock tree, Janet. But that's my point. Neither would you."

"Oh, stop. Now I know why my tummy hurts—it's the stress of your incessant conspiracy suspicions."

"Don't you see the pattern, Janet? First he gets you used to drinking the tea he brings... then he switches to a different brew. And you know what that means."

"Suppose you tell me." Though I already knew what she was going to say. Holly read way too many crime novels in addition to all those TV shows that explored spousal crimes—usually murder. We'd been over this territory before. *Vivid imagination.*

"Look, this is always the way it goes down. When questioned later, after the deadly deed, the neighbors and friends always say they never suspected a thing. Heck, even the other family members never think anything's wrong."

"Once again, Holly, you immediately leap to murder. Is it really all that impossible to believe that Bill simply loves me and wants to show me a little extra kindness?"

"That very quote appears in nearly every episode," she countered, waving her hands erratically. "The relatives and close friends always say the deceased woman just thought the killer husband was being attentive."

"Okay, Holly. Enough. If you're going to turn every conversation about my husband into a thread from all those murder mysteries you overdose on, then Bill Dyson will be an off-limits topic from now on." He probably should have been off limits anyway.

"You can't do that, Janet. I'm the only one who can help you through this treachery. Since you're blinded to the reality, at the very least you need my involvement to protect your life." If not so totally deranged, Holly might have sounded noble.

I suppose my friend's efforts to *save* me from my husband might be comical... except her extreme misinterpretation bordered on being pathological. Well, actually, she'd crossed that border long ago. If I couldn't get Holly off this single-minded capital crime track, it could actually wreck our friendship. And other than her obsession with spousal murders, she'd been a very good friend with whom I'd spent a lot of quality time, even when I was still working full-time. Lately, however, and especially during these weeks I'd been out of work, Holly had been especially frazzled-looking. *Probably not sleeping well.* "Do you remember how much fun we used to have—whether shopping, movies, or just chilling at the coffee shop—before you got so worked up about husbands murdering their wives?"

Completely ignoring my point, she said, "And don't forget, it goes both ways. It's just that the wives killing their husbands is less frequent and usually they'll hire somebody else to do it for them."

"Oh, stop." Feeling a familiar twinge down in my gut, I winced and discreetly pressed my fingertips over the area—lower left quadrant.

"What are you doing, Janet?"

"Nothing. Just a little catch. I told you—it's the stress from all this nonsense you continue to bludgeon me with."

"That's how the poison starts."

"It's not poison, you idiot." It felt a bit like my regular cycle, but that was in a different spot and typically hit closer to the first of the month. "If it's not stress, it's probably just hunger. I'm downing all this tea but not eating anything. You want some toast or something?"

She waved away my offer. "How long have you had these so-called twinges?"

"Off and on... recently." I pointed to the antique wall clock. "I just need to get back to eating a regular breakfast, like I did when I was still working full-time." That had been five weeks ago, and my morning routine was not the only drastic change.

"Janet, I'm telling you..."

"Enough. This is way past ridiculous." I was becoming angry. "Maybe it's best if you leave now. Give me a chance to cool off and provide you some time to think if we still have anything to talk about besides alleged poisoning murders."

She looked wounded. "Whenever the best friend catches on to the plot and tries to warn the victim, she's always kicked out the door."

"Goodbye, Holly. I'll see you tomorrow at the luncheon, but only if you promise to behave and stop this nonsense."

She left without a further word, but was clearly sulking. Even before she'd become so thin and pale, Holly had never liked having her dire warnings dismissed.

A moment later, I looked down into my tea mug, the final few sips now certainly too cool to drink. Saw something swirling around the bottom of the dark pottery. *Hmm... looks like an engorged gnat or something.* Not deadly by any means, but certainly yucky. *Wonder how that got into my tea?*

Stop it, Janet Dyson.

Sometimes Holly had that effect on me—caused me to look at completely normal and typical things, and suddenly find them suspicious. A gnat in my mug just meant that certain tiny insects enjoy tea as much as I do. And I drink plenty. In fact, that was what started this whole thing during my first week, after the layoff—I woke up one day and found that Bill had boiled a kettle of water and already had a full pot of tea steeping, just waiting for me to appear in the kitchen. He'd already left for work.

When he'd gotten home that evening, I'd thanked him with a big hug.

"Did I pick out the right tea leaves?" he'd asked.

Actually I prefer the Earl Grey blend, but I didn't want to dampen his considerate effort. "Yes, the Lapsang stuff is quite nice," I'd answered, with only a slight fib.

"Good," he had replied, "then maybe I'll make it for you again some time. It's a smoky black tea from China. I also found some green chai tea that I'll brew for you. The chai is made from spices, you know, and green tea isn't aged like the black. Should be great stuff. Full of anti-oxidents or something."

"Do all these tea blends come loose in cans?" I had asked.

"Uh... not sure. Why?"

"No reason. Just wondered if any were sold pre-bagged in those foil pouches... you know, so you'd get the exact same amount for each cup you steep."

He'd just shrugged. "Tea is tea. Teaspoon is teaspoon. Anyway, it probably costs more for them to pack it in little pouches."

I'd nodded. *Makes sense.* I kind of wished I *had* emphasized my preference for Earl Grey—which, like Elmwood Inn, I still considered British even though I realized they imported the actual leaves—because from then on, every time Bill made my tea, it was either a black blend from China, a green brew from India, or some other color from who-knew-where (that I'd never tried before).

But no matter. I could tolerate a different type three or four mornings a week. *What's the harm in that?*

⊗∽⌒

October 16—Tuesday—about 10:30 a.m.
SINCE I'D BEEN between jobs for the past five weeks, most of my days were free. In six years of marriage, this was the first time I had not worked a full-time job—the last at the Silver Spur Buffet until our entire crew was laid off with same-day notice and the doors abruptly chained. In an additional bizarre development, the entire structure had been razed within a

month. Made me wonder if somebody was hiding a dead body—*ha*.

I'd begun that job fresh out of college when waitressing was the only employment I could find in my new husband's little town of Verdeville. Even though buffet customers selected and carried their own food, each table still required a lot of interaction. I'd gone from the hectic and lengthy supper shift to the less busy and shorter mid-day shift, and then to cashier, which was significantly less demanding than waiting on the tables.

Now having unstructured days—like the slightly older Holly, who'd never worked out of the home since she'd married her already successful and quickly rising insurance salesman husband—allowed me to get involved with book clubs, garden groups, and an informal assembly of ladies who loved to eat. They had no formal name that I'd ever heard, but I called them the Ditzy Diners. All ages, from my own status of late twenties to a few ladies in their early seventies. I had not yet discerned the exact schedule, but about every three weeks the Diners convened to travel out of town and enjoy a place with real cloth napkins. *And, yeah, that's a treat these days.* Today was my second time to join them and I already knew almost all by sight and quite a few by name. Holly had introduced me and—I suppose you could say—sponsored me into Diners membership... such as it was. At least until I found a new full-time job.

"I was afraid you weren't going to show," said Holly as I exited my ancient Hyundai and trotted toward the sizeable church van that one of the Ditzy Diners was allowed to borrow.

"Always up for a good luncheon," I said, trying to act more cheery than I felt around her at the moment... after yesterday's conversation.

She placed a diet-healthy but painfully thin hand on my forearm. "Are you still upset with me, Janet?"

"Upset isn't exactly the word," I replied carefully. "But the territory you covered yesterday is off limits, period. We'll be fine if we both simply steer clear of that topic."

That truce lasted for the 45-minute drive along I-40 to east Nashville, then through the bustling process of eleven ladies taking seats, indicating our beverage orders, and selecting our entrees from the expensive menu.

"Gosh," I whispered, elbowing Holly as discreetly as I could, "these prices are outrageous. Bill is going to kill me."

Holly's face suddenly drained of blood and blanched even further white. "What did you say?"

Of course, I flushed... deep crimson. It was as though all the blood had wicked from Holly's gaunt face into mine. "Nothing. I mean... just a figure of speech."

"A Freudian slip, if I ever heard one," replied Holly in a hoarse whisper. "And you can't blame me this time, because you brought it up."

If there had been surveillance tape, I would have played it back, because suddenly the woman to my left and another to Holly's right—plus matronly Stella across the table from us—launched into Holly's favorite topic. I felt as though I was dining with the Wives-Who-Suspect-Most-Husbands-Of-Murder Club. Though, curiously, not their own spouses.

"Come on, y'all," I pleaded. "Surely there are more interesting table topics than desperate murders of spouses."

"Name one," whispered Holly, with a hiss. The insurance business had been deliriously profitable for her husband and she lived in the lap of luxury—it completely mystified me why she remained so fixated on murderous husbands. And also why she'd lost so much body weight so rapidly, without being on any known exercise program and only those "healthy" organic foods and supplements.

As Stella and the two other ladies stared at me in silent shock, I struggled to come up with a topic. *Mind is totally blank.* Glancing about the spacious dining room at the décor and hoping that something would catch my eye, I quickly realized most of the other ladies in our group had halted whatever conversations they'd been involved in and now were also staring at me. Not with any sense of hostility—more like bewilderment that I still had not caught on to the universal truth of the cosmos... or something.

"Have you seen what they've done to the place where I used to work?" I asked, figuring that to be a safe topic, since it had been the buzz of the town since the day after Labor Day, when the Silver Spur was abruptly shuttered.

"There was no need for that... treating a historic eating establishment like it was an abandoned shed," said the lady to my left.

Though I agreed with her, I'd hardly considered that buffet to be historic in any way, other than the 1950s plumbing in the restrooms.

"If local investors had been able to purchase it, we'd still be meeting there for brunch," offered the lady to Holly's right. "But they were out-bid by some high rollers from Knoxville. Three Kings, I think it was."

"It was King Three. And I happen to know that some of those big money guys are right here in town," said Stella in a lowered voice.

"Wait," said Holly suddenly, causing everyone to halt in mid-sentence. "We weren't talking about kings tearing down buildings. I was in the middle of explaining how Janet's Freudian slip actually reveals that she's more aware than she lets on about husbands doing away with their wives."

Several heads nodded soberly but no one else spoke.

Becoming more uncomfortable by the moment, I tried to will away the embarrassed and angry flush creeping up my neck. I supposed those ten ladies would have continued—with that same dull expression you often see in the eyes of grazing cows—to stare at me until doomsday, if the waiter had not arrived with the first tray, holding four of the dishes for our table. Food broke the immediate tension of that incredibly awkward moment, but it left my stomach churning and my mind whirling.

With a sharp elbow to her ribs, I ordered Holly to join me in the restroom. "Need to wash our hands after petting Holly's cat," I said weakly, momentarily unsure whether my friend even owned a feline pet.

Looking slightly confused, Holly nevertheless smiled—or tried to—and added something that sounded agreeable without clarifying the status of her own hands or whether she owned any animals.

Once we were safely inside the restroom, I pinned her to the wall near the paper towel dispenser. "What have you told them?"

"What do you mean?" asked Holly, her eyes wide with obvious guilt.

"They know! They all know. You told them everything." At this point the real *everything* in question would be simply that my husband had started brewing exotic teas for me. But I could easily imagine how embellished my saga had become in the inventive and fixated hands of Holly, the maven of Murder Network.

"I only told Stella..."

"Well, obviously Stella told everybody else." I backed up enough for Holly to peel her frail spine away from the restroom's ceramic wall. "Now, how much do they know... or think they know?"

"Just what you told me."

"Ten ladies would not be staring at me like I was a walking corpse if you simply told them my husband has been bringing me tea. Now level with me. What did you say?"

She hemmed and hawed, but basically revealed that she'd discussed with Stella much of the same things she had with me—namely that since "most" husbands were murderers or potential murderers, ergo, Bill Dyson was also. And he'd already tipped his hand with the tea brewing gambit. Then she added, "But we all agree that you're lucky because we caught it early, possibly even before his plans have solidified."

"So you *have* discussed it with the others."

Holly just shrugged. Almost as an afterthought, she began washing her hands.

"I can't believe this. How can I go out there and eat my butterfly Gulf shrimp and stuffed bell pepper knowing that this entire group of ladies thinks my Bill is a killer and I'm soon to be laid out on a cold slab in the coroner's basement lab?"

"Uh, I don't think the Greene County coroner even has a lab," she said, in a strangely detached way. "Somebody said they ship all the bodies to a place in Nashville."

"Whatever. Doesn't matter about the coroner. I'm not going to be murdered and Bill is not a wife-killer just because he brews tea occasionally."

When Stella entered the restroom—as cautiously as if she were a referee at a knife fight—and announced our dishes had arrived, I hurriedly washed and dried my hands and headed back to our table.

ᏆᏟ

AFTER THE REMAINDER of Tuesday's ill-fated luncheon and the deathly silence of all parties on the long drive back to Verdeville, I strode from the church van to my car and drove away without even offering my farewells. In my rear-view mirror, I could see the nine other Diners clustered around Holly and I knew exactly what they were discussing—me and my impending murder.

ᏆᏟ

October 18—Thursday—evening

I HADN'T SPOKEN TO Holly for two full, peaceful days when Bill came home after work with an odd expression on his face. He was later than usual, roughly half an hour. Instead of going straight to the bedroom to remove his suit and dress shoes, he entered the living room where I was monitoring the HGTV channel with one eye and working a crossword puzzle with the other.

"Anything particular going on between you and Holly Salles?" he asked, without any greeting or even a smooch on my cheek. He didn't wait for a reply. "Darren stopped me on the way in and said y'all aren't talking."

This was weird. When did guys even notice—much less care about—an apparent spat between two wives? I shrugged. "Nothing to worry about. Female friends sometimes fall out over silly things. Probably not much different than a spat between you and your buddies."

"Guys don't have spats."

"Whatever you call it. When one of your buddies acts like an ass, so you give him some space to let him work through it and start being normal again."

He was shaking his head. "Doesn't work that way."

"Never mind." It felt like I was on trial here. "So what did Darren tell you?"

"Nothing really. He's just curious why Holly is crying so much. And when we discussed it just now, *your* name came up."

"If you must know, she's gotten on my nerves with all her crazy, um... conspiracy theories."

Loosening his tie, Bill sat on the couch, but on the far cushion instead of the one next to me. "What kind of conspiracy? You mean like the government covering up some captured UFOs?"

"The subject doesn't matter, but it's closer to home than UFOs. I'd warned her to cut it out but she kept right on with all her ranting."

"Ranting?"

By that point, my tears were forming. "Look, this is between me and Holly, and I'm handling it. Okay?"

"Not really okay, Janet," he said with an edge to his voice. "Darren is my friend and if you two are squabbling, it spills over."

"I don't believe this." My chin fell toward my chest. For one thing, I had not been aware that Bill and Darren were buddies.

"So what was Holly ranting about?"

Though my hands were waving in front of me, I was only vaguely aware of them. "It was bad enough that she wouldn't just drop the subject, after I'd told her repeatedly to cut it out. But she'd evidently blabbed everything to Stella and those other ladies at the luncheon. And who knows who else she's told."

"Told what?"

"All her crazy theories."

"For example."

"Oh, Bill... this is not going to end well if you won't drop it. Holly is my friend and I'm handling this. After she has a chance to cool off and clear her head—and stop all her crazy talk—I'm sure we can get back together. But she'll have to shut up about her favorite topic."

Turning to face me, full on, he paused before replying. His cheeks seemed to redden slightly. "Janet, I think you'd better tell me what Holly's favorite conspiracy subject is."

"It'll just upset you."

"I'm afraid I'm already a little upset. My friend complains to me that you've hurt his wife's feelings—when she's already been sick and lost all that weight..."

"So you agree she doesn't look well?"

He shook his head. "I haven't even seen Holly. I was just talking to Darren. Now quit dodging my questions about what's going on." He swallowed hard. "So what's this beef between you two wives?"

I watched his face carefully before answering. I'd never seen him this stern or intense. *Is he jealous that I'm not working outside the home at present?* "Okay, but don't say I didn't warn you. Holly's incessant warnings about a conspiracy... are all about you."

"Me?"

I nodded as I clutched my twinging tummy.

He sat back in his part of the couch and shook his head. "What on earth could Holly know—or think she knows—about me?"

Wasn't sure how to phrase it. "Well, her broader theory takes in a high percentage of husbands, but the specifics relate to her insistence that you, um, wish I was dead."

"That's absurd. You're not yet twenty-seven and your actuarial predicted lifespan would be to about age eighty-seven." He sounded like our neighbor Darren, on an insurance cold call. "You've got a good sixty years to go."

"Uh, Holly's theory involves a certain abbreviation of that actuarial chart."

"Abbreviation? You lost me."

"Murder... all right? She thinks most husbands want to kill their wives and is certain you've decided to do away with me." *There, I said it.*

"Oh... murder. That does explain a few things." Oddly he didn't seem upset.

"So you're not offended that my best friend has spent weeks trying to convince me that I'm the future victim of your foul play?"

"Well, first tell me how the deed is to be done and then I'll let you know if I'm offended. If it's the knotted rope in the library by the evil Professor Plum, that's okay." He smiled... which, with these distasteful circumstances being discussed, seemed tacky at best. "So, what? Push off a cliff? Hunting accident? Hire a hit man?"

"It's so gratifying that you find humor in this bizarre subject." My tone was intentionally icy. "No, it's none of those. Holly believes it will be poison."

"Hmm. That Holly Salles is one disturbed witch," he said, rising suddenly from the couch. Then he looked about the living room as though he'd just then arrived. "Well, I'm gonna get comfortable. You want me to bring you a highball?"

"No, thanks. Not really in the mood." *Besides, my tummy hurts again.* A margarita would be more to my liking, but I didn't want any alcohol to cloud my brain cells while I pondered this development. Holly and I were having a tiff... a van full of other ladies already knew all about it... and now both husbands were involved. And somehow, it seemed every one of them was ganging up against me!

SUPPER WAS WARMED-UP leftovers, which required all the energy and concentration I could muster. Bill was visibly disappointed at seeing the chicken casserole again, but he didn't complain verbally. I went to bed early and tried to read. He stayed up, working in his study on something, and I thought I heard his voice. *Must be on the phone with a work colleague.*

NOT SURE WHAT TIME I'd finally dozed, but it wasn't restful in the least. I woke again around 1:15 AM and Bill still wasn't in bed. After using the bathroom, I went toward the kitchen for a sip of water and paused by the doorway to his study. At first he didn't notice me, so I tried to figure out what would keep him up that late when he had work the next morning, Friday. But the shift of my weight caused the floor to creak and he turned suddenly.

Seemingly at a loss for what to say, he muttered, "Oh, it's you."

Who did you expect? "Just heading to the kitchen. You need anything?"

He shrugged. "No, thanks. Just finishing up this report for tomorrow and then I'll crash."

Without responding, I went to the kitchen, poured enough water for a few swallows, and placed the glass in the otherwise empty sink. *Wonder what kind of report that is?* I thought. The screen he'd had open was clearly our e-mail provider.

October 19—Friday—morning
BILL WAS ALREADY GONE before I rose about eight.

If things had been normal, on a weekday morning I'd likely head downstairs and soon be visiting with Holly and sipping the tea Bill had brewed for me before he left for work. But things were anything but normal—and had been atypical for much of the time I'd been unemployed. For one thing, Bill seemed to resent me being at home, even though he never addressed it directly. Holly had attempted to parse that as passive-aggressive, but I didn't care for her psychoanalysis any more than I did for her obsessions with predicted murders. I definitely *did* feel the absence of Holly's companionship, but decidedly did NOT miss all her ramblings about mysterious deaths and spouses killing each other. *How grim.*

Plus, it was nice to have the house to myself... and quiet. Houses feel different when you're not rushing about to leave for a job. All those years in school and college with classes and assignments, then my six years of waitressing and cashiering—a woman needs a respite from all that chaos and hustle.

Except for occasionally sweeping the floor, I'd rarely entered Bill's small study. He'd owned the house before we married and this was one of the spaces he'd kept as it had always been. Didn't bother me. I had a place for my own books and I didn't need his laptop since I did most of my online activity with my phone or my tablet. Not much in his study but bookshelves, filing drawers, a maple desk, and a small window. Very little on the desk—Bill was a lot neater than I was. Just a few ruled writing tablets and a small notepad. Also some massive books with banking tables—holdovers from the time before computers calculated amortizations and finance charges. A paperback dictionary, and a Bible I'd never seen him open.

More than anything else, his laptop interested me. In the wee hours of the morning, he'd said he was involved in a report for work. Maybe so... but I figured it was more likely he'd been sending or receiving email. *Let's find out.*

I flipped up the lid and turned it on. The home screen came up, but all the accounts and programs were apparently password protected. "That's not too odd," I said to myself, "since bank stuff is confidential." But I had occasionally—albeit rarely—used his email before, when I was sending a file or photo too large and complicated for my phone or tablet. *When was that?* Back when I was still working. Hmm. So the password lock-down was recent. I considered sitting there trying to guess at his password, but my brain was too foggy. Besides, I wouldn't want him nosing around on my phone or tablet.

Pressing the off switch, I closed the lid and slid the laptop back to the spot I'd found it in. Sat there in Bill's study chair and wondered what he'd been emailing about at 1:30 AM. Just as I was rising from the chair, I noticed the notepad seemed to have faint impressions of something that had been on its most recent top sheet. I'd never actually done this before, but I'd seen it often in old movies. I found a pencil in the little round basket on his desk and began lightly rubbing that page.

The image sprang to life almost instantly. It worked! Now what did it say? In block letters, written with a strong hand, it read:

$1M

KING-3

"Must be some bank loan business," I said to myself. "But why would he be messing with this at 1:30 in the morning?"

October 20—Saturday—morning
THOUGH DRESSED CASUALLY, Bill had gone in to work. No lengthy explanation, but he indicated it was an important deadline for a big project and said he'd be back for supper.

That was okay with me. Things had been tense since our conversation Thursday evening and when he'd been home, he was in his study working on a project. Presumably the same one... though he'd had other stressful deadlines before, of course. At such times, it was best to leave him alone and I didn't mind not having to strain my brain to converse.

Mornings—including Saturdays—were just not the same without a long visit from Holly. I would've loved to go over there and make up, but I'd dug in my heels since—through my husband's involvement—I'd started feeling all that pressure from Darren.

Isn't that just like men? Holly and I had a tiff and could've patched it up fairly quickly, but the guys stuck their noses in it and now I felt defiant rather than forgiving. Didn't like the notion of all three of them ganging up on me.

October 22—Monday—early morning
GROGGY AND NONE too cheery, I rose to the alarm at 7:30. Like Friday and Saturday, Sunday had been a blur of coolness and

silence from Bill. I'd never seen him act this way and couldn't believe his behavior towards me could change so much just because I was feuding with a neighbor. It's not like we, as couples, ever did anything together with Holly and Darren Salles.

In the meantime, Bill had also lessened his special attention—vis-à-vis serving me home-brewed tea. And despite their unpronounceable flavors being all wrong, I realized I'd been missing it. Funny how a bit of special attention, some little gesture like hot tea, could feel so warming.

Anyway, I hoped the new week would get off to a better start. I figured to scramble a few eggs before Bill left for work at his usual time of 8:15. But he was already long gone. It wasn't like him to leave for work without eating *something*, even if only cold cereal. But no dishes had been used.

Not wanting to dirty the frying pan with eggs for one, I just hunted in the pantry for some toaster pastries. We were out. Tried to think of something else palatable this early and finally found a partial box of fruit bars. But with my stomach like it had been recently, I couldn't face all that pre-packaged artificiality before a caffeinated beverage to jump-start my nervous system.

What I really needed, besides a margarita (and it was too early for that), was some strong coffee, but I couldn't find any grounds anywhere. *Maybe I'll brew a nice pot of Earl Grey.* But all of my favorite tea blend was also gone. I stared at the small magnetic calendar on the fridge. Hadn't I been to the grocery yesterday on my regular Sunday afternoon run? No, that was when my tummy had been giving me fits. "When was the last time you went to the store?" I asked myself. With no answer forthcoming, I had to conclude it had been the previous Sunday, October fourteenth, some eight days ago. *Or was it Sunday the seventh?* No wonder I was out of toaster pastries, coffee, and my good tea.

But there was plenty of that pan-fired green tea Bill had been brewing for me—well, until Thursday, anyway. I pulled the small metal can from the pantry and set it on the counter. This was actually the first time I'd examined the tea itself. The writing on the label was exclusively oriental characters—not unusual, since the Asians were noted for their teas. I tentatively opened the can. The dried leaves looked shrunken and twisted, a bit like desiccated soldier ants, and they smelled slightly bitter. Hmm. When brewed, it hadn't tasted actually bitter, just not as mellow as Earl Grey. *More of a medicinal taste, I suppose.*

Well, I'd heard about plenty of healthy herbal teas—Asian and otherwise—that tasted medicinal so I figured... what the heck?

Boiled a kettle of water as I munched on the rather dry and decidedly un-fruity breakfast bar. After scooping two spoonfuls of tea leaves into the little metal strainer and placing that into my pot, I added the boiling water. Waited a few more minutes, dipped the strainer up and down a few times, and then poured a cup. I preferred my smaller porcelain cups to the large pottery mugs that my husband had been using for me.

This was a new taste—distinct from its taste when Bill had previously served it and provided its name and description. Maybe it was true that the porous property of pottery mugs actually did modify the natural taste of hot liquids. *Whatever.*

As I slowly drank the rest of that cup and finished my crumbling breakfast bar, I decided it was not healthy for Holly and me to nurse a stupid grudge this long... and figured I'd have to be the one to make the first move. So, after hurriedly washing my hair in the kitchen sink, throwing on some fleece exercise wear that had never witnessed more use than walking to and from my vehicle, I scurried across the street and three doors over, to Holly's house.

Rang the doorbell and waited. No answer. No sign of life when I peeked through the front door's curtained window. Knocked this time. Again, louder. Finally heard a female voice. "I'm coming." She sounded weak.

"Holly? Is that you?" I called louder. "Let me in."

"I'm coming, I said." Sounded like that took all her energy. Eventually she unlocked the deadbolt and pulled in the door just enough that I could see her face. She looked terrible!

"Are you all right? Let me inside."

Finally she stepped back sufficiently that I could enter. I closed the door behind me and beheld the skeletal shadow of the Holly Salles I'd known for six years as her neighbor and friend. "What on earth happened?" *It was only a few days.*

"I didn't want anybody to see me like this. But I'm okay, Janet." She tried to push her stringy hair away from her gaunt, gray face. "I need to sit back down."

When I grasped her elbow to help guide her to the living space, I could feel each distinct bone in her upper and lower arm. "Have you seen a doctor?"

"I thought about it, but Darren says it's just this new strain of flu going around. Knocks you on your butt for ten days before you slowly get back to normal."

If I'd told her how far she was from normal, the fright might have killed her on the spot. "I can't believe you haven't seen a doctor. We need to get you to the hospital."

"Darren says they don't do anything for flu but give you an amped-up vitamin B shot."

"Holly, I don't know what you've got, but it isn't any flu I've ever seen or even heard about." I looked around the room—the place was a mess... and she usually kept it orderly enough to take photos for a magazine feature. "Where's your robe? We're heading to the hospital."

"I can't, Janet. Darren will get angry again. He thinks I'm a hypochondriac."

I couldn't believe my ears. She looked like death warmed over.

"He's been treating me with some herbal supplements he read about on the internet."

"What's he giving you?"

"Can't remember. I've been a little confused for the past week."

"I saw you six days ago. You were fine on Tuesday." *Although rabid about conspiracies.*

"Darren says this herbal stuff has to clean out your system before you feel it working. I guess I had a lot of flu germs to flush out."

I hustled back to her bedroom and grabbed her robe. "Put this on. We're leaving right now. Where's your purse?"

It appeared my question threw her. Finally, she pointed vaguely toward the kitchen. "Maybe in there."

It was. I also grabbed her phone from the counter. "You wait here and I'll go get my car. Be back before you can count to ten." *Assuming she could even count that high in her condition.*

ON THE WAY TO Greene County's modest hospital complex, I asked a few more questions about the herbal stuff her husband had been experimenting with. Holly claimed it was all-natural, mainly herbs that ancient cultures used until modern pharmaceutical companies had hidden—and likely destroyed—all the references in literature and history.

That was mostly bunk and I knew it.

"Darren said if this batch didn't work, that we'll just eliminate it and both move on to something new on that list."

"So he's been taking it, too?"

"Of course. You don't think he'd experiment on me without knowing first-hand how it affects the body."

"So how is he feeling?"

"Oh, he's just like usual. But he'd gotten a flu shot in September, I think.

I ignored the flu topic to focus on the herbs. "Did that particular brew—the one you've been on since Tuesday—also bother your husband?"

"Not sure. He's still on the road. I'll ask him when he gets back."

"Where did he go?"

"Not exactly sure," she replied, her head slumping forward. "I think he said he was driving to Knoxville for something. But I've been a little more confused than normal lately."

The understatement of the year.

I knew my husband had spoken to Darren Thursday evening, because that was when their conversation had caused our big argument. Plus Knoxville was not very far—maybe 150 miles. No reason for him to be gone for days. But I also realized there was no point pursuing any of those matters with Holly right now, as she was barely cogent.

FINALLY WE REACHED the Greene County Hospital at the west end of downtown Verdeville. I pulled into the E.R. entrance, went around to the passenger side, then helped Holly stagger through the automatic sliding doors. Fortunately an empty wheelchair was right at the entrance and I dropped her into it. Rolling her to the admittance desk, I breathlessly provided her name and said I'd be right back after I moved my car, presently illegally blocking the ambulance unloading dock.

By the time I'd moved my vehicle, parked in the two-level garage, and raced back around the complex to the E.R. section, Holly was gone. "Where's Mrs. Salles?" I asked frantically at the desk.

After consulting her screen, the nurse said, "They already took her back."

"Which room... um..." I couldn't think what they called the few curtained enclosures in the E.R. part of our small county facility.

"Are you a relative?" she asked.

"No. We're friends... and neighbors. I brought her in."

"No one besides family is allowed in the examination area," she stated flatly.

"But she needs somebody with her."

"She has," said the nurse, consulting her screen again. "Her husband just rushed in."

"Her husband's out of town!" I replied, far too loudly for the sparsely populated waiting room. "She said he's in Knoxville."

The nurse gave me a pained expression. "Lady, just take a seat. If the family member comes out, you can speak with him."

I SAT. AND WAITED. Tried to get interested in a magazine, but imagined all the germs it had been in contact with and put it back down. Then I trained my eyes on the door which separated the examination areas from this waiting room.

Not sure how it was possible in my state of stress, but I guess I dozed off for a few minutes before awaking with a start. As I was trying to figure out how long I'd been there, a new arrival at the E.R. entrance caught my attention. It was Bill, and he headed straight for me.

"What on earth happened?" my husband asked, sounding more accusatory than concerned.

"I went over to Holly's this morning to try to patch things up and found her in such deplorable condition that I couldn't think of anything but the hospital. I almost called the ambulance."

"You shouldn't have interfered, Janet. Darren has this under control. He said it's that new flu strain."

I wondered when he'd spoken with Darren. "Whatever she has, it's not the flu. You didn't see her—emaciated, with gray coloring in her skin and hardly able to move on her own. It took all her strength just to speak."

He checked his watch, but didn't state the time.

"How did you even know she was here, Bill?"

"Huh? Oh, Darren called me at work."

"Well, for that matter, how did *he* find out?" *And all the way over in Knoxville.* "We'd only just arrived here a couple of minutes before he hustled in while I was looking for a parking place..."

"It doesn't matter now anyway."

"What do you mean?"

Bill paused. "I just mean, now she's getting a professional opinion and her husband is here to comfort her."

"Did you know he's been plying her with some weird treatments he got off the internet?"

"Vaguely. No particulars. Just that they've been sampling some anti-oxidants and probiotics, and a few cleanses or something."

"Whatever it is, it's not helping. She must have dropped twenty pounds in six days, over and above what she'd already lost, and her skin's turned gray. That's not a cleanse."

Bill's shrug totally dismissed my line of questioning. "I'll go check if there's any word yet on Holly."

I sat there, my jaw hanging open. I'd never known Bill to care two hoots about my friend, much less visit the E.R. when she was being examined. *And here he is.* After speaking with the nurse, and the nurse shaking her head, Bill reached in his pocket and showed her something. Looked like a card... or at least something about that size. Then the nurse nodded, went to the back examination area, and soon returned to her seat.

About a minute later, Darren poked his head out the door, my husband hurried over, and they said a few words. Before I could get to my feet and scramble over there, Darren had already closed the door and disappeared. "What did he say?"

"He suggested we go home and he'll call when they know something."

"I think I should stay."

"They're still conducting tests and won't have the results for hours. You need to come home with me."

"I'm in my own car."

"Just come home, Janet. There's nothing more you can do for her."

His wording startled me. "What do you mean?"

"Nothing except what I already told you. Darren said it will take a while before the results come back."

"That's all we know about a woman who was down to maybe 90 pounds and couldn't walk on her own power? No other information at all?"

Bill shrugged. "Home, Janet. I'll follow you."

October 22—Monday—evening

WAITING WAS KILLING me and not knowing made it even worse. Bill never did return to the bank, just stayed home all day and watched me. Felt weird being monitored—last time I could recall such scrutiny was during high school when I was grounded for violating curfew, or some other stupid rule.

Around six o'clock, Bill made himself a sandwich with cold cuts, but I wasn't hungry. Well, actually my tummy did inform me it was empty, but I didn't think I could hold down anything. Instead, my exhaustion—as much mental as physical—sent me to the bedroom for a nap.

By the time I woke, it was after seven o'clock—around eight hours since I'd driven my friend to the hospital. And still I hadn't heard anything. Grabbing my phone, I called the hospital's main desk to learn Holly's status.

"Are you a relative?" asked the lady.

"No, I'm a friend and neighbor. Look, I'm really worried. Just tell me if she's been admitted to a regular room yet." I heard some clacking on her keyboard.

"I'm sorry, we have no room assignment for a Holly Salles."

"Does that mean she's still in E.R.?"

More clacking. "Her file was logged out of E.R. a few hours ago."

"Y'all sent her back home?" I sputtered. "That's nuts. She was barely alive when I hauled her down there."

"Ma'am, you know I can't release any patient information to anyone not on the HIPAA list."

"I just want to know where Holly is!"

She lowered her voice. "Let me put it this way, ma'am. I suggest you contact her family who was with her."

"What does that mean?"

"I'm sorry, ma'am. I have another call." She clicked off.

Throwing my phone on the bed, I burst from the bedroom and stumbled down the hall, passing Bill's study on the way. "Oh, it's you," he said, looking in my direction.

"I just talked to the hospital people and they won't tell me anything except that Holly isn't there any more."

"Calm down, Janet," he said, rising from his rolling chair. "I know."

"You know what? How?"

"Darren called me while you were sleeping. I didn't think I should wake you."

"What did he say?"

"I'm sorry, Janet."

"What do you mean, sorry? How is Holly?"

He cleared his throat. "Darren said she... didn't make it."

"You mean... dead?"

Bill nodded slowly.

"From what? And don't tell me the flu."

"Some extremely rare form of anemia, as I understand it."

"Anemia?" Tears streamed down my cheeks. "If Holly was anemic, it was because of all that herbal dishwater they've been drinking."

"Must be some other cause, Janet," he said, pointing in the vague direction of the Salles' house. "Darren is doing just fine."

When he saw my shocked expression, he corrected himself. "I meant, *physically* okay... relative to their diet and supplements. Of course, he's in a state of grief right now, as would be expected."

My head was swimming. I'd lost older members of my own family before, of course, but Holly was the first friend close to my own age to die, practically right before my eyes. I had to think what the customary actions were, but it was difficult to concentrate. *The family.* "Bill, we should visit Darren... maybe take a casserole or something."

"I can pick up something at the deli tomorrow."

"Tomorrow... right." I struggled to focus. "Well, no need for the deli. I can make something."

"Janet, have you looked in our pantry lately?"

"What?"

"I'm just saying, since we're low on supplies and you're already so, um, distraught... it'll be better for you not to exert yourself."

Exert myself? "A casserole is not at the upper limit of my home-making capability, Bill."

"I know." He gently waved his hands in a downward motion, like he was trying to calm a frightened child. "I'm just trying to spare you the effort. You've been under a lot of strain lately. I sense a lot of confusion."

I couldn't deny either. "Well, I should at least call Darren. He and I were never close, but Holly was my best friend here."

"No, you've had enough of a strain," replied Bill. "I'll take care of it. You go sit down and I'll bring you some hot tea." After filling the kettle and placing it on the stove top, he pulled out a tin of tea leaves from the sparse pantry. He'd noticed me watching. "It's okay, Janet, I've got this under control. Plenty of practice. Go have a seat and put your feet up."

I didn't feel like sitting still or being quiet. I wanted to run down the street screaming with grief and rage. This shouldn't have happened. Holly should NOT be dead. If only we hadn't been fighting, I would've seen the extent of her physical decline sooner and gotten her to professional medical treatment. And as I considered my guilt in the matter, I couldn't even remember what she and I had been fighting about.

I slumped down onto the couch, tucked my feet under me, and stared out the window in the direction of Holly's house. My eyes were naturally drawn toward the TV on in front of me, but my ears were still focused on the kitchen. I heard Bill pick up his phone, hit a speed dial number, wait a moment, and then begin talking softly. "Darren? It's Bill. Just broke the news to her. She wanted to call and see if we could do anything for you." After a pause, presumably to listen, Bill said, "No, she's okay." After another pause when Darren was probably talking, Bill's following words were obscured. Then I heard him chuckle.

As I tried to imagine any part of a condolence call that could elicit laughter, Bill returned to the living space where I was resting, my knees now drawn up tightly against my chest... and tears in my eyes.

"Here, Janet," he said, holding out a heavy pottery mug. "After the shock you've had, I made you some of that special tea you like so much."

END

The Herndon Secret

Charles A. Salter

I HAD FOUR HOURS to get my beloved Sara back... or they would kill her. And it wouldn't be anything so gentle as a fentanyl overdose.

And only Brexxie Herndon could help me now. I stared at him on the far side of my living room, leaning against the wall, shaking slightly and trying to catch his breath. The carpet between us and the sofa were covered in blood oozing from two dead bodies.

Brexxie—short for Breslin. Working for DARPA—the Defense Advanced Research Projects Agency. Said to be smarter than Einstein himself, but now on the lam. Everyone wanted the products sprouted from his intricate grey matter. Everyone: good, bad, or ugly.

"Why did you have to get me and Sara involved, Brexxie? I'm not active any more. You know I'm retired. I have no connections or pull at the Agency any longer."

"Sorry, Jacks. Really, dude. I never thought they'd take Sara."

"That's always your prob, Brex. You live in your own ivory tower. You can't seem to deal with the real world."

"Dealing with it now, dude. Big time. We both are."

"Yeah, all three of us are. If we can't find them soon and free her, Sara is a goner."

"I said I'm sorry, man! When I recognized they were following me, I couldn't think of anywhere else to turn. You were the only one at the Agency who ever treated me like a normal *Homo sapiens.*

I looked at his pale and pasty face, his not quite five-foot height, his almost emaciated frame—from too many office lunches of Peanut M&Ms instead of real food. I knew he had no chance against those thugs on his own, while I, despite being retired, was at least still strong and heavily armed—as the first punk who'd tried to grab Sara had soon learned, a .45 slug between his eyes and his inert grey matter splattering out the back of his head.

"So what secret weapon did you cook up this time, Brexxie? What were they after?"

Brexxie started to tremble. He opened his mouth to speak, but nothing came out. I stepped over the lifeless bodies of Punk #1 and #2—the second with a 12-inch Buck General knife in his chest—and grabbed Brex before he could collapse. The slightest stress nearly always gave him the shakes, or the faints, or the stumbles. He had chosen the wrong line of work after graduating top of his class from MIT... at the age of 16. He should have gone into civilian electronics work and made billions in the private sector world of computers, NOT into Defense work developing new spy satellites, micro-communication gear, and weird personal protection devices for spies.

"No BS, Brex. I don't care if my security clearance expired. You are going to tell me everything, or you and I will die the same as Sara. You got that?"

"Okay, Jacks. Okay. Just let me sit on your sofa for a second and catch my breath."

"So what is it? We're running out of time."

"I call it the Herndon Device."

"Modest as always, Brexxie."

"Well, I invented it, so I can call it whatever I want."

"At least until DARPA puts it in its Top Secret catalogue as part of its new funding request submitted to Congress. By then it'll have a name like 'Personal Protection Device, Microscopic, Electronic, Non-lethal Weapon'."

"Close, but no Havana, *Nicotiana tabacum*. You remember how a hundred years ago, musicians recorded directly on blank vinyl records or even more primitive disks? I'm not talking about recording studios, fancy equipment, or mass production. Just a lone artist or group making a single record in the basement."

"Before my time, but I've seen it in old movies and stuff. A microphone picked up soundwaves from voices and/or instruments, then vibrated a stylus to make grooves in the wax or plastic disk, which spun on a turntable."

"And how did it play back?"

"I think the turntable would spin at the same fixed speed as when recording, and the phonographic needle would follow that same track, the vibrations producing sound waves to be amplified and emitted by a speaker."

"Right," concluded Brexxie. "And my new invention is capable of picking up vibrations stored at the atomic level by any kind of motion and then playing them back as sounds and images of the events which just occurred in that vicinity."

I was stunned. Even for Brexxie, this was a dramatic innovation. "You mean you can get playback of any recent event recorded by objects in this room? Walls, the floor, a glass window?"

"Yessiree, I can indeed."

"You could read off these walls what just happened here?"

"Well, atoms are always in motion, so it is unpredictable how long a 'recording' will last in a stationary object such as a wall. You might get only a millisecond or two's worth of data. But if an object is spinning at a set rate, such as a ceiling fan or a microwave turntable, it makes a longer-lasting change in the pattern of atoms. You can usually get a minute or two of recording before the signal fades."

"Show me," I said. "And where is this thing, anyway? They searched you like school bullies looking for lunch money and found nothing. Where did you hide it?"

"Remember that antique Sasha doll dressed in checkered blue gingham that I handed to Sara when I first arrived? I got it on eBay. A real classic in mint condition. I took it apart and hid the sensors of my Herndon Device in its eyes, the central processing unit in its head, micro-recording equipment in its torso, and the playback screen on its back. Then I put all the doll parts back together again."

"Sara put that doll on the mantelpiece. I'll get it."

Brex continued, "We'll have to take the doll's clothes off to see the screen."

"You always were a perv, Breslin Herndon."

Brexxie took the doll from me, aimed at the ceiling fan, and pressed a button. No sound, but a warm blue glow of what he called Cherenkov radiation shone from both doll eyes. Brexxie then carefully removed the old-fashioned gingham dress from the doll, as one would from a small infant, while humming the tune of *Down By the Old Mill Stream*.

I didn't sing out loud, but I couldn't help but see myself half a century ago in fifth grade, Mrs. Blackwell's class in Ridgefield Elementary School, singing that song along with the class:

Down by the old mill stream where I first met you,
With your eyes of blue, dressed in gingham too,
It was there I knew that you loved me true,
You were sixteen, my village queen, by the old mill stream.

And that brought back a flood of memories of Sara, my beloved, and our second honeymoon, not to Jamaica this time but to the British Isles. Touring a beautiful city with one of the most ancient universities in the world—Cambridge, a renowned educational institution centuries before America was even founded. There we were, punting on the Cam River, when the rains came, and a very chilly breeze, and then blue skies again, then scorching June heat. Sara laughed and said, "I told you England could get all four seasons in one day! Didn't I warn you?"

My heart sang when she gaily reminded me and kissed me on both cheeks, sitting right there on the punt. I would have married her all over again, right there on the boat, right there soaking wet and cold and hot.

Was Brexxie playing with me? He had a habit of elucidating someone's weakness or current psychological need and fiddling with it, almost like a child-god watching ants in a plastic 'farm' cope with the disasters he flung at them, seemingly just for fun. I had seen him play our bosses like that many times over the years, but never one of his friends. Well, his one friend... me. I was nowhere near as smart as Brexxie, but I was smart enough to know when someone smarter than me was manipulating me. "So where is the playback, buddy?"

"Here." He pushed another button, and on the tiny two-inch screen implanted in the doll's back, I could see two living punks walking backwards, with Sara bound and gagged between them, into the room. I saw dead Punk #2 rising up like

Nosferatu from the floor, but with an enormous hunting knife in his chest, then the knife quickly pulling out and rejoining my hand. Then blood, hair, scalp, and skull bits separating from the wall and pulling back into the head of Goon #1 as the bullet returned to my gun.

"It's running backwards," I complained. "Can't you make it play forwards?"

"Of course. The input is received backwards, with the last event playing first, and everything else in reverse order until the image simply fades. But I can record it and play it forwards." Which he then did.

I complained again. "We already know what happened here. How does this help us?"

"Patience, my dim-witted friend. *Bleibe ruhig, mein kind.* I was just proving to you that it worked. Now we scan for images with possible clues as to where they were taking Sara."

AFTER TRYING WITHOUT success to get a good scan off numerous surfaces within my bungalow, Brexxie finally got a good read off the sidewalk where the hostage van had apparently parked.

He played the vid forward this time. I could hear the goons mutter about their destination at the Bel Arch—a reproduction in Manhattan City Hall Park of the archway entrance into the ancient Temple of Bel, or Baal, from Palmyra, Syria. It had been in all the papers and TV and radio talk shows. The whole of NYC was abuzz with the idea of re-creating part of an ancient pagan temple in modern America.

In Brex's vid, I could also see Sara's helpless, terrified eyes, and rage coursed through me like a tsunami. I wouldn't even need weapons to handle these two. I could tear them apart with my bare hands.

But first we needed to find them. And I'd better bring weapons—lots of weapons—in case those goons had plentiful allies.

I looked at Brexxie, rapidly growing impatient as he oh-so-carefully replaced the blue-checked dress on his prized possession.

He still seemed more fixated on the dress than on our immediate problem. "You know, gingham is made from cotton, species name *Gossypium hirsutum*. Nearly pure cellulose. The most commonly used natural fiber throughout the entire world for thousands of years. Over twenty-five million tons are produced globally per year."

"Brexxie, ol' buddy, Sara is on the verge of death and you are giving me a science lecture. I'm about to snap your scrawny, brittle pretzel neck in two..."

"Patience, my friend. *Bliebe ruhig.* Or as your Agency peons and drinking buddies might mutter on the fifth beer in your stupid pidgin Latin, '*Hastus makus wastus*'. I'm trying to make a point."

"You have three seconds and then it's going to be *breakus yoo neckus*, if we're not burning rubber peeling out of here to the Bel Arch!"

The tiny shrimp of a man looked genuinely alarmed, as if realizing he was pushing me too far. "Proceed to your Cadillac EL at once, dear Jacks, and I shall continue my disquisition on the way."

I dashed to my EL in the driveway, opened the trunk first, and pulled out more weapons. My Colt .45 semi-auto had jammed after killing #1, so I had tossed it on the floor rather than clearing the round, what with #2 leaping upon me at that very instant. Now I pulled out my Taurus Judge .45 Long Colt/.410 shotshell revolver, my Ruger Blackhawk .357 Magnum revolver, and a petite .380 semi-auto for Brex. The latter was a little girl's gun; Sara always complained if I handed it to her when we went hunting or target shooting. Like me, she preferred Magnums or at least specialized high-caliber shells for their superior stopping power. I'd learned that in my early training days at the Agency—not Breslin Herndon's Agency, but my own, one he knew little about, the one which had assigned me to protect him while he worked at DARPA.

I had plenty of stopping power in my Judge. The revolver only held five cartridges, but each was a shotshell with nine large pellets rather than a single bullet. "Can't Miss" ammo, I called it, though after decades on the firing range and occasional real field use to save my life, I rarely missed any man-sized target within about 100 feet.

I offered the little Beretta Pico to him.

Brex looked askance. ".380? With Cor-Bon Jacketed Hollow Point rounds?"

"But of course."

"A 90-grain bullet with a muzzle velocity of 1,050 feet per second? For me?"

"You can handle it, Breslin. Even preteen girls can shoot that thing."

"That's 200 foot-pounds of energy. Have you ever heard of Newton's Third Law of Motion? 'For every action there is an equal but opposite reaction.' That much recoil energy will knock a little guy like me on my ass. I barely graze the scale at a hundred pounds when dressed in a full suit and heavy leather shoes with heel lifts."

"Then brace yourself before you fire. Get the round off and fall back if you must. Better to plunk on your rear than have one of those goons slice your head off."

"Point taken. I would rather bash my sacrococcygeal joint than part with my caput."

Once I got his scrawny ass in the car, him still fiddling nervously with the Beretta, I did indeed peel rubber and squeal tires. We were in the middle of Long Island, and it was a long drive to Manhattan.

And Sara needed me.

⌒~⌒

THEY WERE WAITING for us, of course. Not simply at the Temple of Baal arch, where I expected massive opposition, but after we had gone no more than two blocks from my house.

I saw the glint of sharp steel in the sun and realized it was a trap—tri-cornered spikes lay scattered on the road to take out my tires. And they did, both front ones exploding loudly before I could slam the brakes and squeal to a stop, the car pivoting around 'til I was facing back the way we had come. Then the right rear tire came to a final halt just as it, too, met a sharp spike, exhaling in a final gentle pop.

From a dark van just around the corner ahead darted two more goons straight for us, CQB rifles at the ready.

I looked over at Brex. He was still swooning from the violent halt. He had dropped his pistol and had both arms extended, trying to brace himself on the front dash and the passenger door simultaneously. He looked shaken but not particularly afraid, more like someone on a roller coaster than in a pond surrounded by alligators. "What've you got that can stop fully automatic rifles, Brex?"

"Not to worry, my dear friend. This should do it. Hold your ears for a second, then put your Magnum to good use when they drop their rifles."

From a pocket in his vest, Brex pulled out a little whistle-shaped object, pressed a switch on its side, lowered the window, and tossed it toward the approaching duo. He immediately raised the window and clapped both hands to his ears, as did I.

An ear-piercing shriek burst forth from the device for a couple of seconds. It sounded like a cross between a train whistle, tugboat foghorn, and exploding jetliner all at once, and up close. It made a flash-bang hand grenade seem like a quiet whisper.

The goons dropped their rifles and fell to their knees, faces in agony, hands clapped to their ears.

I popped open my door, stood on the pavement, and shot one goon in the forehead, and he collapsed to the street, hands relaxing from his face even as his legs gave a final shudder. I shot the other fellow in the chest and he fell backwards, hands still in place, still breathing. *Must have missed the heart; my aim is off.*

Brex recovered his Beretta from the floor of the EL and cautiously walked towards the still living punk, while I darted to the van to see if it held any more goons or, with luck, Sara. But I doubted that, for these two were not the pair who had left our house with her.

As I got close to the van, the driver leaned out his window and fired two rounds at me with a handgun, then floored it, trying to get away. I ducked, then knelt in the street to brace my arm for a better aim and fired the Blackhawk four more times as the target gradually shrank in the distance. I know I got the rear windshield, but the van kept moving.

I returned to Brex's side and muttered, "Scan 'em."

"Already scanned the dead guy. Nothing. Just a couple of seconds of seeing through his eyes as he approached us a bit ago."

"How about the other turd?"

"He's still alive... still moving... it's going to ruin the scan."

"I can fix that." I holstered my empty 'hawk, pulled out the Judge, and with one shotshell turned his head into hamburger.

"Geez, Jacks. Now you destroyed all the tracks. There's nothing left for me to read."

"Sorry. Didn't realize the limits on your device. Let's go and see if we can catch that van. I think I slowed it down by shattering the rear windows and maybe hitting the driver.."

On foot, we caught up to the van in less than a minute. It was crashed into a STOP sign, the driver crumpled over the wheel. *Guess I did hit him through the window after all.* Cautious about him playing possum, I poked his neck hard with my still-hot gun muzzle and then felt for a pulse with my other hand. Nothing. I tossed his body to the pavement.

And nothing else of import in the van. Just some boxes of 5.56mm NATO ammo for the CQB rifles.

Brex did a scan, just in case. All we got was a scene of my four rounds hitting the vehicle and it careening out of control as the driver lost consciousness.

I could hear sirens approaching and knew we didn't have time to deal with the police. "To the Bel arch, then?" I stated more than asked, while taking the bloody wheel of the terrorist van.

"To the Temple of Baal, the original of which saw countless human sacrifices."

As we drove off, I headed west for Interstate 495 from Long Island to Manhattan. Eyes on the crowded thoroughfare, I asked him, "So what were you trying to tell me about gingham and cotton a few minutes ago?"

"Oh, yeah, it's my theory about who and what is behind all this and why."

"Go on."

Brex looked as happy as a teacher with a captive audience and a big story to tell. "The French word for gingham sounds like Vichy, the city in France where many experts think cotton was first turned into gingham. You know about Vichy, right?"

"Something about them starting a government there to collaborate with the Nazis during World War II after Hitler invaded and knocked out the Free French government in a matter of days."

"A-plus, Jacks. Sometimes your intellectual prowess surprises me."

I took that as an insult, as intended. "So... cotton, gingham, Vichy, collaboration with the Nazis. In the present realm of reality, where is your train of thought heading, Brex?"

"What we have here is a failure to—"

"—communicate?" I volunteered.

"Don't go all Strother Martin and *Cool Hand Luke* on me now, Jacks."

I shrugged. "*Independence Day* would be a more timely allusion."

"No, what we have here is a *pons asinorum*."

"Okay, Brex, I know you wrote the classic textbook on Latin as a freshman at MIT, but not all of us have read and memorized it. Explain, professor."

"The *pons asinorum* is the point at which most people fail any longer to follow a logical argument or explanation of a theory and just intellectually quit."

"Oh! You mean like politicians and bureaucrats!"

"Well, now you *are* catching on. Maybe there is hope for you yet, Jacks."

Another sarcastic insult. He was playing me again. *I wish to God he would play our enemies like that.*

He continued, "Most people, when confronted with something they can't understand, simply fall back on dogma, slogans, or personal attacks rather than even try to plow through towards understanding. For instance, you try to explain to a leftist that socialism has been not only a spectacular failure anywhere and everywhere it's ever been tried, but a horribly twisted and sadistic mess causing impoverishment, destruction, and death for hundreds of millions of people—"

I interrupted, "—but instead of waking up and trying to understand reality they just call you names such as 'greedy capitalist' or 'capitalist running dog' or 'racist.' I see what you are getting at there, Brex, but still not how this ties in with who is up against us now."

"Well, Jacks, I'm at a loss for words at this point. I don't yet have the exact names for our enemies in this caper either, but just as the Vichy regime collaborated with the enemy and were rightly seen as traitors by the Free French, some elements in our government must have turned traitor, released secrets, and are trying to undermine what you and I and other patriots want to preserve for future generations."

"So you think we are facing not an outside enemy but rogue elements from our own side who have access to all the secrets we have?"

"Indubitably. Who else would look at me and recognize me as the secret Brainiac behind all of our recent spy satellites? No one outside our Agency knows me at all. I'm just the pathetic little egghead walking down the street that no girl will look at twice."

I thought of my beloved Sara and the joys of our romantic relationship, and for the first time ever realized just how lonely Breslin Herndon had to really be. It wasn't just the negative attention from the male bullies and insensitive dolts that I had always recognized and often tried to protect him from. It was also the absence of positive female attention and companionship. "That would also explain why none of these assailants so far look foreign or are speaking a foreign language. They are as American as you or I."

"Well, perhaps in terms of location of birth and growing up. But as far as I am concerned, you can't loathe America and despise most of its citizens and want to destroy our current system and yet still consider yourself a *real* American."

I glanced at Brex and smiled for the first time that day. "Brex, you may be the smartest man in the world, you may know millions more things than I do, you may even know nearly everything there is to know... but I know the three most important things, and it seems you do, too."

He looked back at me and met my eyes. "God, family, and country."

"Yes. God, family, and country—in that order."

I got off the 495 at Flushing Meadows and headed towards Grand Avenue in Queens. The light ahead turned yellow, so I brought the terrorists' van to a halt at 57th and Grand. A dark van pulled up to my left, another to my right, and then a van facing us on the other side of the intersection ahead swerved out of its lane, ran the red light, and smacked head-on into my vehicle.

Before I could respond, some goon on my left smashed my window with a crowbar and tossed into the vehicle a small ball-shaped thing which fizzed and emitted heavy smoke.

Just as I was passing out, I saw men wearing gas masks emerge from all three vans.

I GRADUALLY CAME TO with a pounding headache and a sour taste in my mouth, but knew enough to keep my eyes closed. I could hear traffic sounds and feel the floor on which I lay bumping on a rough road surface. Couldn't sense whether I was alone or not.

I carefully tensed my arm and leg muscles to see if I was still all there. Nothing seemed to be missing, but all four limbs were bound at my back, and I was lying on my right side. Couldn't tell if I was bound by ropes or some kind of cuffs.

I eased my eyes open a crack and found myself staring at legs dressed in black, tactical ops garb. There was a low-slung holster on the right leg with a dark pistol in it, just inches from my face, but no way for me to grab it. Ditto for the boot knife on his left leg.

Suddenly I heard Brex moaning. He had to be coming to also and feeling as bad as I did. The legs next to me moved and I heard a couple of footsteps, then Brex's voice.

"Let go of me, you ape!"

The only reply was a snort of derision.

I opened my eyes wide to see a lone goon standing upright and holding Brex with one hand, completely up in the air, as if he were a large ham or sack of potatoes. His arms and legs were unbound and flailed helplessly in the air.

Clearly they didn't see him as a physical threat. Didn't even tie him up.

Brex looked quite unhappy and was shaking, his eyes darting wildly about the enclosed space. He seemed to catch sight of my awake eyes, but gave no tell-tale sign nor call for help.

Finally he found his tongue. "I see right through you, hollow man."

The other man just grunted. More than twice Brex's size and bulk, he shook the pint-sized man in the air like a bulldog shaking a bone.

"I can take one look at you and know exactly what kind of girlfriend you have. She's a masochist who loves it when you give it to her hard and rough."

The bulldog growled and dropped Brex to the floor of the van, where he landed with a pained grunt.

But the little man wouldn't give up. "When you get mad at her, do you like to rough her up all the more like a good little sadist? No, I don't think so. I think you withhold sex to really punish her, to NOT give her what she wants. You are a twisty-diddly little perverted sadist who can't even play your sadist role straight!"

The goon took a step closer, bent down to Brex, and clasped a hand around his throat. "Don't talk about Mona like that! I'm warning you!"

"Mona, oh, Mona, you moan-a so well in the throes of passion when bully boy here can finally get it up. Moan, Mona, moan. But he's not man enough to get it up most of the time, is he? He's a pathetic, impotent, little limp worm who can't give you what you want!"

Then Brex started to gag as the hand around his throat squeezed tighter.

A dark look fell over the punk's cross face. "Lucky for you Mr. Derrick won't let me kill you. He wants your secrets—all of them. But a broken bone or two won't keep you from telling all. In fact, it might even help loosen your tongue."

The goon let go of Brex's neck, but then bent low to grab his arm with both hands, like someone grabbing a wishbone.

Brex looked at me, desperation in his eyes.

I yelled, "Right leg—pistol!" as I reared back and kicked with all my force into the punk's jaw, relaxing his hold on Brex's scrawny arm and knocking his head into the rear door of the van with a loud crash.

Brex slickly withdrew the pistol, flicked off the safety, and blew Mona's boyfriend to where he needed to be.

But I watched in horror as the recoil blew Brex into the air and hard against the side wall of the van. He collapsed to the floor, eyes closed.

The blast was enormous in that enclosed space, and my ears rang with pain. We had maybe three to five seconds before the driver stopped and came back to check out what happened.

"Brexxie! Left leg, knife!"

My diminutive friend didn't move. His eyes remained shut. The van screeched to a halt.

I reared back again and smashed the goon's head against the back of the truck a second time, hearing a satisfying crunch as the cranium collided harshly with solid steel.

I could see my binds now—PlastiCuffs. A couple of seconds with a knife, and I could free myself. I rolled over—painfully in that position—towards the lifeless body, stopped with my back to him, and tried to slither down to where my bound hands could reach his knife.

As my finger tips began to graze the knife's pommel, I could see the rear cargo doors beginning to open and hear someone outside grunt, "What happened, Palsie?"

As the doors fully opened, swinging one to the left and the other to the right, I could see another goon standing there with pistol drawn.

Our eyes met and I could tell he instantly recognized the essence of what had happened.

As he raised his pistol aim towards me, I slipped the knife out of its sheath and held it firmly as I kicked the lifeless body of Palsie into his partner.

That knocked him off balance, but only for a second.

I rolled to the van door and through it, twisting and kicking so that I fell backwards into the live man, the knife pointing backwards also and plunging somewhere into his torso.

I could hear the pistol clatter to the street as he let out a restrained grunt.

The knife had plunged deep, and within milliseconds my hands were covered with his blood. But he wasn't out of the fight yet. I twisted the knife and tried to dig deeper, but he boxed my head with both fists and then went for my throat. I could see stars.

Brexxie began to moan and look around in confusion.

"The gun!" I choked out with my final breath.

Brexxie picked it up and pointed at the mug choking the life out of me. Then he shook his head. "No, I can't take that recoil again. This is a 9mm, way more powerful than the .380."

Calmly he sidled over to us struggling on the pavement, me trying to cut some essential artery with the knife before I blacked out and it was all over.

Brexxie raised his hands high and swung them down as if holding a sledgehammer, smashing the pistol grip into the goon's face.

The grip on my neck didn't lessen. Brexxie wasn't strong enough.

I thrashed left and right, loosening the grip on my neck slightly and digging the blade into any flesh it would reach.

Brexxie hit him a second time. A third. The punk was strong and highly disciplined, but not immortal. The cumulative weight of all his wounds began to take their toll.

I wrested free of his dying grip and rolled off him, just in time to see Brex jam the pistol muzzle into the gunsel's mouth and brace the butt against the man's sternum, so that his own body would absorb the recoil.

Brex pulled the trigger, blew most of his caput off, then took the bloody knife from my hands and cut my bindings loose.

⌒

IN THE FRONT SEAT of the van, as I drove, Brexxie got some good readings with his time scanner. A solid 83 seconds of the plans they had discussed. We knew exactly where the van had been headed, what they had intended to do with me and Sara, and how Breslin Herndon would be working from now on for their boss, Mr. Derrick.

"There's just one thing I still don't understand, Brexxie," I said. "Why do they want to sacrifice Sara at their new Temple of Baal? In primitive Baal worship, they just sacrificed children, didn't they?"

Brexxie chortled. "You mean you don't know?"

"What do you mean?"

"I realized it the moment Sara opened the door to let me in, over an hour ago now. The fresh sparkle in her eye. She didn't tell you?"

"Oh, you mean...? That little imp. I guess she was planning to surprise me with the news at just the right time."

"I guess. You may think I am the smartest man in the world, but I'll never understand women. My brain is simply not on the right frequency."

"Oh, they're not that complicated, Brexxie," I mused. "All women want the same thing; the problem is they can't have it."

"What do they want that they can't have?"

"A man, a good and solid man, that they can then mold and change into perfection."

"I see," said Brexxie. "He may well change, but not necessarily in the ways they want."

"Exactly. We get set in our ways, develop a paunch, and don't want to do what we don't want to do."

I glanced at Brexxie and he looked thoughtful. "I have observed that many times. So what do men want?"

"Also something they can never have."

"Namely?"

"A good and decent woman who *won't* change over time, who will always remain young and attractive and responsive."

Brex stroked his bony little chin. "Jacks, sometimes you honestly do surprise me with your wit. I tend to think of you as a big, strong ape—a valiant silverback gorilla, if you will—someone loyal to a fault, with a big heart and true love for the good in humanity... but who can stomp the crap out of any errant or rotten banana."

"Good one, Brexxie." At last an honest compliment. *I think.*

"But, dear Jacks," continued Brex, "though you have posited a profound dichotomy, it is an artificial one, and like all dichotomies it subsumes too much. Not everyone fits neatly into one of only two categories, all one or the other. Human variability is too great for that."

"Point taken, Brex. But I find it a useful rule of thumb in most cases, even if not always fully applicable. And why do you always call me Jacks, with an S on the end? You know my real name is Jack Rigalto."

"I thought nicknames were a sign of affection in your macho spy world. Besides, that makes your name rhyme with mine. I like it when best friends' names rhyme."

I looked at him in surprise. "We're buddies, right? Don't make me punch you."

"Alpha male all the way, you silverback gorilla, leader of your troop, righter of wrongs, protector of females and the young."

I laughed. "You were pretty alpha yourself back there. Thanks for saving my life."

"That's what best friends—I mean good buddies are for, right? You've saved my life plenty of times."

I steered the conversation back to our current problem. "And now we've got *two* people to save... plus trying to keep our own asses alive."

"I do like that addendum. I'd like to see all four of us make it through this."

"We will, Brex, we will."

"More alpha posturing. Now that we know his name—Derrick—suppose I told you I just figured out who our enemy really is, and if I tell you everything all at once you won't believe it. This is the biggest conspiracy in the history of the modern world, and you are going to think I'm a nut. Your gorilla mind won't be able to grasp the enormity of this plot at all."

"So walk me through it step by step."

"First, have you noticed no cops are chasing or trying to stop us since we took over the rogues' van?"

"Now that you mention it, yes. We've passed several cops while zooming down Grand Avenue towards the Williamsburg Bridge, but none seem interested."

"That means this vehicle is registered to one of the many enterprises controlled by Mr. Derrick, the man these rogues work for."

"The reclusive billionaire and physicist?"

"The same." Brex looked off, way off into the distance before continuing. "He makes the old reclusive billionaire of yesteryear, one Howard Hughes, look like Miss Congeniality by contrast."

"And the police won't touch his cars?"

"Not those nor anything else belonging to him. If some innocent bystander sees those two bodies we left back at that intersection and phones in our license plate, the moment a cop runs the number he'll see it's on the Do Not Stop list. He'll figure it belongs to one of the foreign consulates around here and not bother us unless the consulate itself—or really, our Mr. Derrick—phones in a problem."

"So what else do you know about this ringleader?" I asked.

"Derrick is no doubt the second smartest physicist in the country... second only to myself, of course."

I guffawed at that. "Modest as always, Brex."

"It's not vanity when you tell the truth, Jacks. Have you ever heard of the Seven Millennium Prize Problems?"

"Negatory."

"The Clay Mathematics Institute offered a prize of one million dollars to anyone who could solve one of the great puzzles of mathematics that had stumped the experts for centuries. I solved one, only to discover Derrick had independently solved it as well... but finishing a day later than I did, without yet learning about how I did it. The Institute split the prize and gave us each half."

"So what did you and Derrick solve?"

"There is literally no way I can explain it where a gorilla like you can understand it. You won't understand even the name of the problem."

"Try me."

"The Yang-Mills Existence and Mass Gap problem." Brex chortled and looked at me expectantly.

I took a big breath and held it. Then I slowly exhaled. "Moving right along. So you two have been enemies since he stole half your prize money?"

Brex shrugged. "I couldn't care less about money as long as I have enough for a roof over my head, clothes without holes, and plenty of M&Ms to eat. You know the three things I do really care about and have devoted my life to—God, family, and country. And you and Sara are about the only family I have left now."

"But you're sure your Derrick and the one this goon was talking about are the same bad guy?"

"Of course. He's the mastermind behind CERN."

"That's the lab in Switzerland with the largest particle accelerator in the world? The Super Hadron Collider?"

"Yes. Mind you, none of the public knows the Derrick connection, and none of the public figures working in CERN realize who their primary benefactor really is. They just think it is European governments funding them."

"So maybe it is. In any case, that's just a scientific lab doing science. There's nothing evil nor malevolent about that."

"Of course not," continued Brex. "Not the science *per se*. It's the plans of Derrick for the uses of that science that concern us."

"Namely?"

"You know from the news how a little bit of their real intent leaked out? They claimed they were looking for the God Particle. The media took it as a silly nickname or physicist injoke... only it wasn't."

That blew my mind. "What the heck is that? How can a particle be a god?"

"Well, obviously it can't. The proper name for the particle is Higgs boson, postulated decades ago by Higgs, and recently demonstrated actually to exist by experiments in the Hadron Collider."

"Skip the physics mumbo-jumbo and tell me what's the connection with a god, whether a joke, nickname, or whatever."

"Here's where we delve deep into the ultimate conspiracy theory, the one you simply won't believe."

"Try me."

"The particle isn't a god, but Derrick wants to use this research to become a god, all-powerful and in control of the universe."

I let out a low whistle. "That *is* the ultimate conspiracy," I concluded. "A real-life James Bond villain who wants to become not king of the world but master of the universe?"

"Exactly."

"I don't believe it."

"I knew you wouldn't. Your mind is too finite to grasp infinite concepts, but I can give you an example or two you might understand."

"Go ahead."

"How do you think some of the CERN folks celebrated their great founding of the Collider?"

"With boring political speeches that put the audience to sleep?"

"Nope."

"With fireworks and news media galore, and the audience waving flags of all the European countries which contributed?"

"Nope."

"With a super-expensive luncheon for the top science and governmental elite? Beluga caviar, Dom Pérignon Rose Gold Champagne, and lobster thermidor?"

"Three strikes and you're out. With first, the installation on-site of a statue of Shiva, the Hindu god of destruction; second, an orgiastic costumed neo-pagan dance at the opening of the Gotthard Railway Tunnel not far away; and then third, a mock human sacrifice at CERN in the middle of the night to summon the power of the gods, or god particles, or whatever supernatural powers they think they can thereby access."

"Scientists turning neo-pagan? Dabbling in the occult? At work?"

"Well, not the principal scientists. But the folks who know the real intent behind everything are going full-bore occult. I know you won't believe any of this, but look it up online later if we survive all this. You can see the pics and even video of the pagan orgy choreographed at Gotthard in 2016—a horned and fur-covered Satan figure surrounded by six hundred actors, many scantily clad, dancing worshipfully around him."

"But you say that human sacrifice at CERN itself wasn't real?"

"Right. Just a dry run. Derrick is planning the real thing tonight at the newly installed archway entrance to the Temple of Baal in New York City Hall Park."

"So the most advanced scientific minds in the world— some of them, at least—have gone full circle and returned to the most elementary pagan roots of mankind. Why?"

"Well, the particle isn't a god, but Derrick believes the marriage of ultimate science to the occult will turn *him* into a god. Romans 1 foretold all this two millennia ago: 'Claiming to be wise, they became fools...'"

"If Derrick is all-powerful, who can stop him?"

"He's not all-powerful; he just thinks he is. That is his Achilles heel, his fatal flaw. We—you and I—are the only two people in the world right now who can stop him. You, the most valiant and true-blue ex-agent in the country..."

"...and you," I added, "the smartest man in the world."

"Plus we have the greatest possible motivation. We must save your family—our family—whatever happens."

"Game on."

I PARKED THE VAN in an alley on the north side of City Hall, a couple of blocks away. Derrick's crew had to know by now that we were coming, but I hoped we would have some control over timing our approach and might still have some element of surprise in how we encountered them.

I turned to my small friend, who looked more determined than ever. His body might be slight, but it held not only a great brain but a heart to match. "You got any more surprises in your bag of tricks, Brex? Any more of those noisemakers?"

"Yes to tricks. You know I always have something up my sleeve. But no to my ear-piercing Devil's Whistles. That was the last of those I had on me."

"What's our plan?"

"We separate here. You seek out and free Sara, while I find and distract Derrick."

"*That's* our big plan? I could have thought of that."

"Which, dear Jacks, is exactly why I chose it—something your limited mind could understand. My initial thought was to use the Chylon maneuver from Zartu three-dimensional chess. But the first step involves you throwing a psychnet over the whole of the Manhattan PD, and I figured by the time I explained everything to you, Sara would be dead. Would you rather go with Chylon?"

"I'll find Sara," I steamed, and stalked off.

"Wait!" groaned Brex. "You don't know the code word yet."

"What is it?"

"137."

"What's that?"

"The so-called magic number in theoretical physics."

"I don't get it."

"You will when the time comes."

I headed out again.

"One more thing, dear Jacks. Remember some of the OPFOR we're facing now are completely innocent. They have no idea who Derrick and the rogue agents are and what they are up to. Guys like this are just honest cops, City Hall guards, detectives... maybe even a SWAT team later... folks just like us who are just doing their duty. We don't want to be hurting any of them."

"How am I going to be able to tell the difference without a score card?" I wondered out loud.

"If you're close enough to one, look at the eyes. A rogue agent will have a hardened, knowing look. He's in on the plot and knows he works for Derrick rather than whatever agency pays his salary and which supposedly he works for. But an honest cop will have a look of uncertainty in his eyes, for he will suddenly be thrust into a situation he has no prior knowledge of."

"Great. Meanwhile, how am I supposed to keep the good guys from killing *me*?"

"Glad you asked. I almost forgot to give you one of my secret weapons."

Brexxie handed it over. It fit nicely into my hand, and I instantly knew what it must be for.

Brex pointed to a button on the top of the grip. "Press here when you're ready... and make sure you don't point it at me or Sara."

"But it's non-lethal?"

"Sure... if you use it right."

Knowing we had to be under surveillance, I watched as Brex cautiously wandered off to the left of City Hall, closed to the public by now, its workday done, while I eased off in the other direction.

The sky was clear but growing dark, and the yellow and golden leaves of autumn fell rustling to the park grounds with every gust of wind. Then I realized what Brexxie had been getting at when describing the occult ceremony about to go down this evening. Today was the autumnal equinox—the Mabon Festival in the neo-pagan Wheel of the Year, and that night was a full moon, a harvest moon, just rising above the horizon over the Hudson River. *Of course... Derrick saved his occult ceremony for the magic night of Mabon.*

I had reached the grounds of the park and could see the front steps of the City Hall building when I first noticed a handful of uniformed NYPD guards. They likely knew nothing about us and posed no threat until the action started. Then they would no doubt take me and Brex for terrorists.

A couple of hundred yards away, I could see the outline of the Palmyra Arch of Baal's Temple not far from the park's circular fountain. *Why on earth did the global elites pretend they were just preserving art when they placed reproductions of this symbol of evil in London, New York, and scores of other cities around the world? If art, they could have chosen the Palmyra City Gate or the statue of a Roman emperor. By supporting Baal, they were deliberately inviting in untold evils of the universe, not celebrating ancient art.*

Suddenly a commotion arose by the Arch, with a couple of dozen people clambering about a makeshift stage right in front, setting up lights aimed at the Syrian marble reproduction.

As I drew nearer to the 20-foot tall replica, I suddenly realized why they had reproduced only the entrance—they didn't need the whole Baal Temple, for Derrick planned for the city itself to represent a temple of sorts, and this entrance served his occult ceremony as the one by which he would summon the evil spirits of yore to pass from their unknown dimension through this entrance, into the modern world of humankind.

The ultimate marriage of future and past, of advanced science and the most elemental superstitions from the beginning of time. And somehow with the addition of blood via human sacrifice, Derrick believed all this power would install itself within his person and make him a kind of god.

I was no expert in theology, but I knew Derrick was on a fool's errand. He was falling for the oldest and most common of all the Devil's false promises, that by submitting to him, a human being could become like God himself. Only when it was too late would Derrick realize he had sold his soul for a vain and empty promise.

If things progressed that far. Brex and I were determined to prevent this sacrifice and ceremony... or die trying.

Then I saw her—my beloved Sara.

My blood boiled as I saw two strong toughs lead her to the center of Baal's Arch, fastening chains to restrain her there. She seemed very frightened, yet still able to keep herself from falling apart. She looked like Fay Wray set outside the village gates as a human sacrifice to appease King Kong, but was not all hysterical and screaming. At least not yet.

I began to sprint towards her when four rogues leapt, ninja-like, from the trees above me and fell to the ground into a circle around me.

The first one I mistook, out of the corner of my eye, for a falling branch and instinctively ducked. This saved me, for he initiated a powerful roundhouse kick as he sailed through the air, but it missed my rapidly moving head. I came up from my crouch with two fists straight into his chin and knocked him out cold.

By then the other three stood in martial arts crouches, warily assessing me and where to strike.

Before they could think it through, I lashed out simultaneously with a kick at the one to my rear, and retrieved my Judge with my right hand and blew away the rogue on that side with a single blast, and pulled out Brex's stun device with my left hand and sent a pulsating wave of hypersound into the last assailant's chest.

That fourth man looked as if a charging rhino had rammed its enormous horn into his chest. As his body flew up into the air and backwards several feet, his chest itself undulated in and out so rapidly I could not count the times. He couldn't even breathe and collapsed into a clump on the park's lawn.

A police whistle sounded sharply, and half a dozen uniformed guards dashed towards me.

Rogues or innocents?

Before they got close enough for me to see their eyes, I heard Sara scream, "Jack! It's a trap!"

She distracted me for a crucial tenth of a second, and I momentarily forgot I had merely kicked the rogue who landed behind me. Before I could realize that he was on his feet again, he grabbed me in a chokehold around my neck with his left arm and fiercely tugged on my hair with his massive right fist to pull my head back.

I rammed my right elbow sharply into his ribs, and he gasped for air but didn't let go.

I rammed with my left elbow while simultaneously curling my right foot around his leg and jerking forwards to trip him.

His grip on my neck loosened, but I could still see stars from the lack of oxygen-filled blood to the brain. Next thing I knew, he was falling backwards to the ground and I was falling backwards on top of him.

Then six NYPD officers loomed over us and all grabbed me at once.

I couldn't see all their eyes as they dragged me towards the Arch, but the youngest patrolman had a naïve look.

Before I could speak, my assailant in the recent tumble regained his footing and muttered curses as he ran towards us from behind and delivered a sharp blow to my right kidney.

I swooned and thought I would throw up, but they ignored him and kept dragging me towards the Arch and its stage.

On the center of the stage stood a curious figure, thin as a rail but perhaps seven or more feet tall. He had some kind of weird helmet or headdress on his head which I didn't recognize.

Then Brexxie emerged from the shadows of trees nearby and made a beeline straight to the stage.

Sara saw him, too. "Run, Brexxie! It's a trap! Save yourself!"

He kept his eyes on the stage and waved for her to be silent. "It won't work, Derrick. And I can prove it. Listen to me before it's too late."

"So you appear in the open at last, Comrade Breslin Herndon! I've been tracking you on my screen all this time, watching as you pretended to disappear into the shadows and sneak around like a spy. I laughed at your simple-minded re-enactment of a toddler playing hide and seek. Soon I'll be able to see all even without my drones, cameras, and electronic devices. I'll be the Universal Eye with my own power!"

"No, you won't. I can prove it to you, right here and now, with mathematical precision."

"I call bullcrap, Comrade Breslin."

"It's simple, really," said Brex in an ominous tone. "137."

"The fine-structure constant has puzzled and vexed physicists for two hundred years. And you expect me to believe you've finally figured it out?" Derrick hooted in derision.

"I'll explain it to you right here and now," maintained a determined Brex.

"Go ahead."

"The number 137 provides the ultimate key to linking Einstein's theory of relativity, electromagnetism, and quantum mechanics into a grand, all-encompassing universal field theory."

"All that I already know."

By this time, the gang of officers had me on the stage, and now Brex stepped up on it as well. For the first time, I could see my petite friend side-by-side with his nemesis, who was equally thin but seemed nearly twice as tall. *Mutt and Jeff*, I thought.

"Feynman had it all wrong," asserted Brex. "So did Paul Davies and especially Laurence Eaves. Larry claimed this was the number which could be used to summon intelligent alien life from other parts of the solar system."

"Which is exactly why I have embedded 137 into every facet of this project. The Arch is 137 yards from City Hall, I've mounted 137 lights on stage to turn on all at once at exactly 137 seconds before the end of Mabon. I will prolong the human sacrifice for 137 seconds, sending the child's immaterial spirit into the ether at the precise conclusion of the autumnal equinox."

"And it won't do you any good."

"Why?"

"In your zeal, lust for power, and eagerness, you left out a key calculation."

"What?"

"You assume that the aliens with whom you have been in contact are corporeal beings like ourselves, but from other planets or galaxies."

"Of course they are; they've told me so themselves. And tonight they arrive at the stroke of midnight and we shall all see them for ourselves! After which we'll dispose of you and your dim-witted friend here, Jack Rigalto."

"And it never occurred to you not to trust these alien beings?"

"An advanced super-race from another galaxy? Capable of inter-galactic transport? Why should we not trust them, especially you and I, Comrade Breslin. We are the two most advanced of our race, and we shall meet tonight the most advanced emissaries from another one. And they'll make me a co-prince of the universe."

"Why shouldn't you trust them? Because they are not corporeal beings, and you will not interact with them as a corporeal being yourself. They will convert your mass into energy via Einstein's greatest equation and interact only with you in a non-physical, non-temporal realm."

"What on earth are you talking about?"

"You think yourself so intelligent that my dear friend Jacks here is but a worm, a bacterium in contrast to you. But even he knows what these beings are, a fact so crucial to the next phase of your existence."

Brex took his eyes off Derrick for just a moment and turned to me. "Tell him, dear Jacks. Who is he inviting into his life this night?"

I looked at Brex and thought him the bravest man I had ever known. Risking everything to stop this monstrous plot and save my family—our family—from this power-mad fiend. I looked at my beloved, still chained and waiting to die if Brex and I failed. She still looked scared but also had hope in her eyes and a sense of fierce determination not to give up. Finally I looked at the tall, gaunt figure whose eyes now gleamed with the expectation of momentarily receiving absolute power.

And I told Derrick the truth, straight out and unvarnished: "They're not physical creatures who evolved independently on another planet somewhere across the cosmos. They're immaterial beings who have always been here since before the dawn of human time... they're *demons*."

Derrick stared blankly at me, like a tall, thin tower about to collapse.

Brex broke the moment of stunned silence. As he pulled another of his special tools from his pocket, he announced grimly, "And you don't need all this rigmarole and human sacrifice to meet them. All you need to do is shed your mortal coil and join them on their plane of existence. I'll prove it to you."

Then Brex pointed, squeezed some kind of trigger, and Derrick vanished in a puff of acrid brown smoke... leaving nothing but a tiny quantity of grey ash where his shoes had been.

In the ensuing confusion among the crowd, I twisted free from the grip of my captors and rushed to Sara's side.

She looked disheveled and exhausted, but not in the least panicked. I knew her, the woman I loved and admired, and she had the strength of ten, the fortitude to face anything life dished out and stand tall and proud to the end. "They were going to kill us, Jack!" she shouted above the din on the stage behind me. "Both of us. I'm—"

"I know. Brex told me." I started to undo her shackles when she screamed in warning.

I turned around to see the rogue who had sucker-punched me when six armed policemen were holding me down.

He had a maniacal gleam in his eye... and a SOG Government-model knife in his right hand. "I don't know what your partner did to the boss, but we can still kill your lady friend here... and her little brat. Then you'll be next."

"I doubt it. I think you'll be joining your boss Derrick on his final odyssey in another couple of minutes."

I got down into my fighting crouch. He only had a knife, it seemed, but I had a gun... but in my holster. If I went for the gun, he would strike before I could retrieve it.

So I faked him out. I pretended to reach for my sidearm while stepping back out of blade range.

The moment I noted him tense to spring forward and slice open my chest, I dropped the pretense and leapt towards him, bringing up both arms. With my left I blocked his thrust, ramming the tendons in the elbow so hard that he lost control of his grip and the knife fell to the ground.

With my right hand I grabbed his hair, as he had done to me, then whirled down and into him, throwing him off balance and pulling him over me in a judo throw.

He sailed into the air and landed on the ground five or six feet away, chin first.

I sprang upon his back and gave him a revenge rabbit punch.

I had thought to spare his life and let the police arrest him, so that we'd have a good witness in case he decided to turn state's evidence. But by this time, Sara had finished releasing her shackles and bounded over to give him a good kick in the ribs.

She owed him that... it was nothing compared to the 137 seconds he was going to spend making her die in order to fulfill Derrick's fevered plan.

But she wasn't fast enough withdrawing her leg. He twisted to the side, grabbed her foot while it was in the air, and shoved, forcing her backwards and off balance. Then he tried to twist and throw me off him while extending his fingers, claw-like, toward both my eyes.

As she fell towards the ground, Brexxie sprinted forward and caught her before she could injure herself.

I was in no mood to fool around with this creep any more. I had tried to show him mercy, but he attacked me and Sara both even when it was clear he had nothing to gain.

Before he could scratch out my eyes, I pulled out my Judge and fired into his head just above the ear, nine pellets sending him to join Derrick's new kingdom.

"Thanks, Brexxie." Sara laughed as she regained her balance and stood upright.

I got up, too, and looked around. The good police, the naïve but dutiful ones, seemed to have caught on to who was good or bad without a score card. Or maybe Brex had been able to explain things while I was contending with this goon.

Whatever the reason, the cops were mopping up the final half-dozen rogues and arresting them.

I turned to Brexxie and laughed also. "Brex, you are my true brother-in-arms. I haven't discussed this with Sara yet, but I know she'll agree. We want you to be the little one's god-father."

Brex smiled. "Me?"

"Sure. You're family, right?"

"Right." He leaned over to give me a hug.

I pulled back. "Don't make me punch you, brother."

He laughed, but his eyes now seemed moist. "You alpha, you."

Sara changed the topic. "I'm starved. Eating for two now, you know. Brexxie, can you join us for dinner? I can whip up a big bowl of M&M Peanuts in no time."

"Yum!"

I hugged Sara and we walked off towards the van arm in arm. Brex walked on her other side and tentatively placed an arm up high over her shoulder.

"It's okay, Brex." She smiled. "I won't punch you."

Brexxie beamed.

Sara brought the three of us to a halt and looked at him. "Once you become little Sara's godfather, though, I'd like you to help me fix Jack. He needs a lot of changes before he becomes a real father. He's got to give up cigars, for one thing."

I and Brexxie exchanged knowing looks. "No, Brex, as god-father you've got to help me. I don't want Sara so exhausted as a new mother that she forgets who I am and starts to ignore me."

Still looking at me, Brex broke into a huge grin. "You know, Jacks, for a gorilla, you're pretty smart after all. I take back everything I said before."

My grin grew as well. "You know, Brex, I think this is the beginning of a beautiful friendship."

"Right you are, Bogey. Right you are."

END

Time Conscious

J. L. Salter

August 1999

EVERYBODY WANTS TO know about what I now call "The Incident"—which happened six weeks ago. But whenever I've shared that experience without the proper context, people just don't seem to get the full impact. When the TV people were here, all they wanted was a twenty-second sound bite... and they kept interrupting me to ask questions. Finally, I just had to tell them to leave. So unless you have the time to hear the whole thing, I'd rather not proceed.

You *do* have time? Good.

Funny thing about time. Though I'd always been super-conscious of time—and hardly ever late for my shift or for any significant deadline or appointment—after I'd retired, time seemed to hardly matter much any more. So it was quite a puzzlement that I'd even noticed how my bedroom clock slowly, but steadily, crept into the future.

Yes, I mean that literally. Oh, I know you're thinking, "Duh... her clock is fast and gains a minute every so often." I get that a lot. Sometimes to my face, but easy enough to detect with the raised eyebrows, the more blatant eye roll, the sideways *looks* at any other person who might be present, or the muffled snickering as I leave a room. Go ahead, I say to the skeptics, laugh.

I wouldn't even be taking the time and effort to record this explanation with you now, if not for the little girl next door—Harmony—who showed me kindness, attention, and affection. She was the only one since I retired who gave me *her* time, and the only person of any age who actually believed the mar-

121

velous phenomenon we'd jointly discovered. Yes, I trusted little Harmony with the bizarre mystery of my bedroom clock creeping into the future. I don't know how much she told her parents, but I doubt she even tried to communicate it with the few friends she had in her own age range. People look at you funny when you reveal things you know about before they happen.

So, if I have your interest and you won't interrupt for the next few minutes—assuming you have the time—allow me to explain what was going on one late afternoon about ten days before "The Incident." That was six weeks and ten days ago... make a note.

Ready?

My name is Elizabeth Prater, but the little girl next door calls me Miss Lizzy.

∽

FOR THE REST OF this to make much sense, you may need to know I was an administrative secretary in a large public library for a long and steady career up through 1991, by which time every member of the administration had their own personal computers and did most of their own typing and revising. Oh, I still had plenty to do—mostly clerical tasks by then—which was considerably below both my training and my experience. Anyway, they finally just took away my electric typewriter—on which I could still produce 95 words per minute, by the way—and told me to learn the software program which worked those new PCs.

Suffice it to say, I was already old enough to retire and had the requisite number of years to take a pension of nearly 90 per cent of what I was earning—so why kill myself with software? Why, indeed. I'd been widowed for six years by that point, so there was nobody I needed to consult with. My decision and mine alone—which was fine with me. Also, my time and mine alone... to do with as I pleased.

You haven't done much fidgeting yet, so I take you for a different kind of audience from what I've become used to. I'm glad. Because you'll be one of the few who gets to see the whole picture once we arrive at the The Incident itself.

Anyway, I took my pension and moved here to Verdeville. We're still in the city limits, but close enough to the interstate that I can reach the road to Nashville in a matter of minutes. Between us and the highway are acres and acres of trees which usually buffer normal highway noise. It's peaceful out here in this older, but still quite nice, residential neighborhood. There aren't all that many houses on this particular curve and hill of Millrose Drive. The place next door would usually stay rented for a year—which was evidently the term of lease—and then be vacant for a few months before a new renter moved in.

I'd been retired for approximately eight years when the Canada family moved in next door. That would've been about the beginning of 1999, I suppose. I'd wave and try to be friendly, but they kept to themselves and I rarely saw them. Can't say this for certain, but I sort of figured being African-American made them a little bit more cautious in their new surroundings than perhaps a typical Caucasian family might be.

Bear with me a bit longer. For The Incident to make sense, I need you to understand how I came to know little Harmony. Okay? Good.

Mr. Canada worked about half a mile away and he usually walked each way unless the weather was bad. I later learned that was so his wife Natalie would have access to their single vehicle if any trouble arose. He enjoyed the exercise, I was told, and apparently stayed in excellent condition, judging by his stride and speed. Being on foot, he could pace himself exactly and was never slowed by traffic snarls or other road problems. I'm not positive where Tyrell Canada worked, but it might be a bank—someplace with very regular hours and he was a stickler about his schedule.

I rarely saw mother or daughter leave the house and the little first-grader was never allowed in the front yard by herself at all, as best I could figure. The school term had not yet begun and the only reason I got to know Harmony was that Natalie knocked on my back door one afternoon. In my whole adult life—as best I can recall—I hadn't let any visitor in my back door. It took me a second or two to even realize it was Mrs. Canada from next door. Back then I didn't know her first name.

Anyway, Natalie was distraught with some sort of emergency to tend to and couldn't reach anyone else to babysit her daughter. I didn't realize it at the time, but later learned the sole reason she knocked on my door was because I was the only Millrose neighbor who'd ever greeted her or even waved. But, sure, I was available to sit with Harmony for a few hours. I loved kids. I hadn't been around children all that much, though, having had none of my own. I enjoyed being an aunt and great-aunt to the kids and grandkids of my brother and sister, but that exposure was limited, as you'd imagine, since they all lived in another state. They all called me Aunt Lizzy.

Unlike younger children—who might be frightened by a stranger—or older ones who'd perhaps be reserved, Harmony seemed immediately to adopt me as her great-aunt and we fit together perfectly. After I'd told her how my nieces and nephews addressed me, Harmony immediately began calling me Miss Lizzy. When Natalie came to pick her up later that same evening, Harmony begged her mom to allow her to come back and visit me often.

Though Natalie seemed uncomfortable at that moment, she soon loosened up and gave tentative permission, provided that Harmony was home before 5:40, when her father arrived from work. Oh, and she also stipulated that Harmony always went from her back door to my back door, never entering either front yard. I didn't comprehend the importance of that proviso—maybe she was afraid of kidnappers or something—but it didn't bother me to use the alternate entrance. Soon I just left my back door unlocked. In the waning weeks of summer, it wasn't long before Harmony would come over nearly every weekday morning for tea and some little dessert I'd made. And nearly every weekday afternoon, if I was home, she'd come over to play a silly board game or to have me read her a story. Those visits were beautiful moments and I treasured them.

Let's see, I may have gone down a rabbit trail. Ah, yes, the reason you came today. I was getting to the point of explaining how I noticed that my bedroom clock had crept into the future. Actually, it was little Harmony who noticed first. She'd been given strict instructions to be home by 5:40, when her dad arrived on foot from work and paused at their mailbox for Harmony to run out and meet him. I'd watch from my front window as he'd lift her up and let her collect that day's mail and then they'd walk hand in hand up the sidewalk to their front porch, where Natalie would greet them as though they'd both been gone all day. That was the only time I ever saw Harmony in her front yard.

Where was I? Oh, yes. Now I've brought you up to the point about ten days before The Incident—which is when I found out about my bedroom clock. In my living room—where we usually visited, unless in the kitchen—I'd been reading Harmony a funny story and I'd laughed so hard that tears were in my eyes. When I went into my en suite bathroom to rinse my face, Harmony followed me into the bedroom. When she saw my digital alarm clock, she shrieked, "Oh, no, I'm nine minutes late. Mom's gonna kill me!"

Sure enough, my clock indicated 5:49. I tried to calm Harmony and reassure her that no harm should come to her for being a few minutes late, just that once. Then I volunteered to go home with her to explain to her mother that Harmony was late only because she was comforting me—thinking my tears were real. That was a little fib, but close enough to truth that I figured it would hold up if Harmony was questioned further on the matter.

So we hurried, hand in hand, from my rear door across the two yards to her back door, and Harmony hustled on in, all a-flutter with apologies to her mom for being late. Then she pointed to me, standing outside on the rear stoop. Natalie opened the door and allowed me inside, then said, "What's all this about, Miss Prater? Harmony isn't late. It's just now—" and she checked two of her kitchen clocks "—5:37. She's home with three minutes to spare."

"Oh, good," I said, sighing with relief. "By my clock, she was nine minutes late and she was afraid she'd be in trouble."

After Natalie shooed her daughter toward the front door to watch for Tyrell, she turned back to me and shrugged. She noticed me eyeing her kitchen clocks and checking my own watch. All were within a minute of each other.

"Well, I'm glad she wasn't late," I said. "Meeting her dad every afternoon is obviously very important to them both."

After a nod from her and the following awkward silence, I made my excuses and returned home. Natalie's reaction puzzled me. She didn't seem nearly as time-strict as Harmony had led me to believe. But more important than the reaction of my neighbor was the matter of how and why my bedroom clock had gained so much time. I mean, if you figure it took Harmony and I at least two minutes to race from one house to the other, that indicated my clock was at least eleven or twelve minutes fast.

Remember, I said earlier that I didn't pay much attention to time in my retirement years, but I was also not in the practice of having my household clocks telling the wrong time. After all, I never missed the beginnings of my favorite shows, and I always left the house in time to get to church, medical appointments, and meetings of the Homemakers group I was involved with.

You're being patient and I appreciate that. As I said, you'll better understand why all this background is important once I get to the part about The Incident that shook the entire neighborhood—which won't be long now. Is your tape machine still running? Good.

So I examined my bedroom clock, reset it to be in sync with my watch and the other clocks—kitchen, living room, and even the spare bedroom, which I only used when the nieces and nephews visited with my siblings. Oh, and the clocks built into the oven, microwave, and coffee maker, of course.

Having done that, I put it out of my mind and went on with my slow-paced life of retirement.

It was Harmony who later called my attention to the fact that my bedroom clock again read differently from my others.

THOUGH SHE'D NOT been back for at least two days after that *I'm-late* episode, Harmony returned mid-morning on the third day and joined me for tea. Mostly milk and sugar in hers, of course. Sometimes she was quite the chatterbox, but that morning she kept walking to my bedroom door and looking at something inside that space. When I inquired, she merely shrugged and said, "Just checking. Your clock in there is still different from these others, you know."

I thought it was extraordinary for a child that young to even be cognizant of clocks or the concept of being early or late, much less able to read both digital clocks and the older styles with a face and hands. Someone had taught her well—likely her time-conscious father. But I didn't pay much attention to her observation until after she'd returned home.

Checking all my other timepieces, I determined each was within one minute of all the rest. But my bedroom clock had gained well over four minutes just since I'd re-set it three days ago. That's over a minute per day. And I'm not talking about a timepiece with a mainspring that's too tight, either—this is a digital display clock plugged into the wall outlet and backed up with a nine-volt battery. How on earth could an electronic clock gain so much time that quickly?

Anyhow, that was the third morning. Later in the evening, I was bringing some freshly laundered towels to the en suite bathroom when I looked over to the north-facing window and saw a blinding flash. Lightning had struck the utility pole at the corner of my property and the vacant lot to my east.

If you've ever seen a power line transformer get zapped, you can picture the loud boom and all the sparks. And of course, my power went out, as did all the neighbors' I could see across the street and to my left. For no particular reason, I made note of the time—which, because of my battery backup, remained on with my bedroom clock. It was 8:32. That time possibly stuck in my head because I once had a friend who lived in my high-rise dorm when I was a college student. She lived on the top floor in room 832.

Yes, I'm getting to the point. Please bear with me.

Well, the bedroom and bathroom had gone dark, of course, because of the power outage, so I grabbed a little pen-light I keep in a lamp table drawer near my bed. Turned it on and made my way toward the living room. As soon as I stepped through the door, I could see that all the house lights were on, including the bedroom I'd just left.

That's odd, I thought. But maybe it was one of those situations where the electric company could bypass that downed line and route power to our part of the neighborhood by some other circuit. I didn't dwell on it. Crisis over... power restored. Then I pulled a few more clothes from the dryer, poured some juice to drink, and sat down to watch my show—one of those British comedies. It came on at 8:30 and I still had a minute to spare.

Then I thought, *Wait. How could it be 8:29 when several minutes ago, it was already 8:32? Didn't make sense. Oh, well, I thought, that's just the bedroom clock gaining time, as it's done lately.*

127

So the show starts, we get past the introductory teaser thing, the credits start running, and then BAM! Out the north living room window, I see a blinding flash of lightning and the transformer explodes again.

Again? I thought. *How could a transformer explode twice? Once it's dead, it's dead. Right?* As I hurried closer to the front window, I noticed the time on my wall clock—8:32. Now, you need to know that my living room wall clock is the most accurate of any of the timepieces in my house. It's always right on the money with the time hacks shown on the cable news shows and the weather station. So how could it be 8:32 again?

Opening the front door, I looked up and down the street. It was already past dusk, but still light enough to make out a few people peering from their porches as I was. Didn't see any of the Canada family, but I could tell one of their front curtains was parted. So, basically, everybody on my end of Millrose Drive was now aware of the lightning strike and exploded transformer... which I'd witnessed twice. The first time at 8:32 from my bedroom, the second time, just now, also 8:32, but from the living room. I didn't make note of the exact difference, but evidently at least four minutes apart.

I was still adequately dressed to venture forth, so I hurried across the street to the elderly couple whom I occasionally spoke to, but we'd never developed a relationship. I say elderly and you smile. What I mean is they're older than me. So let's say they're in their eighties. Anyhow, I asked them how the transformer could blow out twice, roughly four minutes apart. The husband—can't recall his name, maybe Owen something—said, "It wasn't twice. Just once, and just now."

Well, I chalked that up to maybe Owen being so deaf that he couldn't hear an explosion 65 feet from his front door, or feel the ground shake from the lightning strike. Went back inside and would have watched the rest of my show, except the power stayed off for most of that half hour.

That was the first instance and I call it Pre-Incident Number One. That was the third day, remember, since we learned about the odd time-keeping of my bedroom clock.

On the fourth day, Harmony joined me for tea in the morning. I'd made some little strawberry tarts and she gobbled them down. I didn't want to bring up the subject of the previous evening's explosion because I didn't want to worry her. And I didn't have to; she mentioned it.

"That big bang last night scared me," she said. "I spilled chocolate milk on my PJs."

"Startled me, too, Harmony," I replied. "I was putting away towels for the first boom and watching TV for the second one."

"What do you mean, Miss Lizzy? I only heard one bang and after I changed my PJs, Mom went on and put me in bed since it was dark in the house."

"So you didn't hear the second noise, about four minutes later?"

Harmony shrugged and eyed the plate with more tarts. "No, just one."

"So you must have fallen asleep quickly and just dozed through the second one."

"No, ma'am, Miss Lizzy. I was wide awake, because I knew it wasn't time for bed even though it was already dark inside."

I guess you're able to follow this, right? I now had two separate witnesses tell me there was only one boom and flash, whereas I'd seen two. One from my bedroom at 8:32 and the other from my living room at 8:32, but roughly four minutes later.

Well, I'm not crazy—I know what I saw and when. The trick now would be to figure out what all the variables were. And as you've likely already guessed, it was all about either the clock in the bedroom or the bedroom itself. At first I considered just moving the clock, or maybe replacing it completely. But for some reason, that gave me a profound sense that I'd never learn the mystery behind this phenomenon unless I let it play out to a logical conclusion.

So over the next few days, I made it a point to venture into my bedroom at times I normally wouldn't—after all, who needs to hang out in their bedroom if they live alone? And on those occasions, I'd look out both the north and west windows to see what I could see. Then, if anything stood out, I'd make careful note of the time. That west window faced the Canada house, but nothing happened in front except the mail delivery at the curb. And it turns out mail delivery was at the heart of Pre-Incident Number Two.

On that sixth day since noticing the clock issue, I happened to be in my bedroom when I heard a dog bark somewhere down Millrose and saw through my west window the mail being delivered next door. It was 1:27 PM—which is within the typical two-hour window that our postal delivery lady usually arrived on weekdays. I wasn't looking for any mail in particular, but I get plenty of catalogs and they're diverting to leaf through. So I went directly outside, walked down my sidewalk, and flipped open the box. Nothing. *Hmm,* I thought, *wonder why I didn't get at least some junk mail?*

Didn't think much more about it and got occupied in the kitchen with something. Must've been nearly eight minutes later that I heard a neighbor's dog bark. Went to the front window in the living room and there was the mail lady, bringing mail again to the Canada family. And this time, she also stopped at my box. I hurried out to catch her and arrived just a few seconds after she'd rolled away. But she saw me and backed up with her *beep beep beep.*

"Something to send out?" she asked.

"No," I replied. "Actually I just have a question. Maybe it's none of my business, but how come you made two runs today, just a few minutes apart?"

Shaking her head, she squinted her eyes nearly shut. "Huh?"

"I saw you come by the neighbor's just a few minutes ago, and when I checked my box, there was nothing here." I made the motion as if it would help. "And now you're back. This time you stopped at my box."

"Lady, this is my first and only time on this route today. Even if I missed something, I wouldn't be able to double back, because it screws up my timetable and I get chewed out by the tyrant at the main office."

"Oh, okay." My forehead must have scrunched up. "And nobody else ran this route today?"

"Nope. My route, unless I'm too sick to drive. And I'll probably die on this route, because all the good routes are occupied by the drivers with more seniority... most of them men, of course."

"Of course."

"So you don't have any mail going out?" she asked.

"No. Sorry to hold you up." I waved. "And thanks for stopping."

Without further comment, she checked her dashboard clock and side mirrors and hit the accelerator.

I can see from your expression that you're catching on. There was a time differential between what I could see outside from my bedroom windows and what I would see later from a slightly different angle from any of my other windows facing the same direction. And that differential grew by a bit more than a minute each day.

Now I could tell you about other verified incidents if we had time. And I didn't even officially count that incident which I *heard* from my bedroom window—it was a multi-car pileup on the highway just beyond those woods behind my house. In that situation, I heard three distinct sounds like *WHAM WHAM WHAM*—though not equally spaced. Checked my bedroom clock and it read 8:05; I was still in bed. Less than ten minutes later, I was in my living room watching the eight o'clock morning news from Nashville and that particular station had a news truck that was filming something about the morning commute heading west toward Nashville. They were live and the time hack showed 8:05 as the background traffic went *WHAM WHAM WHAM* and the reporter ducked. Then the anchor lady said something like, "Wow, guess our videographer's gonna get a Pulitzer for that live shot. Are you two okay?" And you're likely wondering why I'd leave that one out. It's because even though I heard it from my bedroom, I didn't see it and I wasn't able to confirm with anybody I already knew that it didn't actually happen twice, about eleven minutes apart. Understand? Okay.

Now, to save you the tape and time I won't explain about Pre-Incident Number Three on the seventh day and Pre-Incident Number Four on the ninth day—I'll just move straight to The Incident itself, the one which started all the media attention on me. Assuming you're ready and you've still got the time.

TAPE STILL GOING? GOOD.

After the double lightning strike on Day Three and the double mail delivery on Day Six, I was more than a little frightened, I don't mind telling you. But I was also intensely curious. I'd already assumed that I might never know HOW this was happening, but I continued to focus on WHAT was going on—you know, in case anyone like you ever came around wanting to know the whole story. And yes, I'll let you see my clock in a little bit, provided you promise not to touch it. Frankly, I don't know what would happen at this point if anybody messed with it.

So, back to my story.

Pre-Incident Number Three on the seventh day and Pre-Incident Number Four on the ninth day were both just as starkly contrasted as the first two pre-incidents. And, as with the others, these two had additional witnesses—from outside my bedroom, of course—who'd sworn the situation in question had occurred only once. No point in debating with either of them. I knew very well what had happened and I kept careful notes.

By Day Ten—remember, this was ten days since we'd learned that specific clock kept its own time—the bedroom clock was close to twelve minutes fast. *Fast* is what the TV people said. But I know, and hopefully you will soon understand and believe, I was truly seeing twelve minutes into the future. But only from those two bedroom windows.

So here we are—six weeks later—finally examining Day Ten. And this is The Incident itself —what you've been waiting to hear about.

Harmony had been over for tea, as usual. Other than the first episode with the transformer explosion—which she had come to believe was actually two explosions, as I've maintained—I hadn't quizzed her about any of these additional matters. She hadn't brought them up, either. But she did continue to check my bedroom clock periodically and would always remark on how much time it varied from the ones she could see in either my kitchen or living room. When she'd do so, I'd just nod and smile and act like it didn't concern me. I didn't want to worry her, you see. Furthermore, I couldn't let myself fixate on it—such could drive anybody crazy.

Well, Harmony went on back home after our morning tea. By the time three o'clock rolled around, I'd expected her to reappear and had a story all picked out to read to her. But no Harmony. Four o'clock and she still had not showed. Finally, it was nearly five and I heard her knock at my back door. She was all excited to show me the new shoes she'd gotten that afternoon. Her mom had taken her shopping downtown, which puzzled me slightly, in that I hadn't heard their vehicle leave or return. No matter. Things were allowed to proceed along that stretch of Millrose Drive without me observing every single one. Right?

I admired her shoes and she chattered about their shopping trip. Mostly little details that stick out to young children but which adults either don't notice or wouldn't care about. I knew we didn't have sufficient time remaining for a game, but thought I could still squeeze in a little story, if I could get Harmony to run out of steam telling her news for that day.

She did quiet down, finally, and we settled in the big easy chair in my living room. I was enjoying the story as much or more than she was and didn't pay any attention to the time. Since she needed to use the bathroom, I sent Harmony to the guest bath, and while she was engaged in that, I decided to do the same in my own facility. I'd just washed my hands and was passing through the bedroom when I noticed it was 5:36—four minutes until her father would arrive at their mailbox with his long, precise, healthy strides.

I started to call out from my bedroom and tell Harmony to head for the back door, but I thought, *Wait, this is the bedroom clock. Since it's a dozen minutes fast, that means she has plenty of time to get back home.* So I just stood there, one eye on the clock and one eye on the street and curb at the Canada house. I'd seen their loving embrace and cute ritual with the mailbox on many previous occasions, of course, but only from the front living room windows. After all, I'm rarely in my bedroom at 5:40 in the afternoon.

When that clock reached 5:39, I heard a loud engine roaring and a screeching noise—tires squealing—and suddenly there came a bright blue muscle car from the late 1960s. Couldn't discern the make or model, but that didn't matter, because it was traveling at high speed around this curve and down the hill of our end of Millrose Drive.

My breath caught in my throat as I saw Tyrell Canada approaching with such a stride and momentum that he hardly hesitated other than to turn and look toward the screech and roar. Within an instant, Tyrell was at his mailbox, Harmony was rushing to him, and the out-of-control car was careening directly toward them both.

133

With a scream, I flung myself from the bedroom to the living space—my heart pounding—yelled for Harmony to come to me... and I jerked open the front door.

No sign of anyone or anything amiss.

Struggling to control my panic, I reasoned: with the twelve-minute difference between those two rooms, 5:39 in my bedroom equated to 5:27 in the living room. So I should have a dozen minutes to get outside and warn Tyrell not to go near his mailbox.

When I turned back inside to look for Harmony, I must've whacked my head on the edge of the door—and I blacked out. Not actually unconscious and it wasn't me in a true faint. Just momentarily blotto. When I was fully cognizant again, I checked the living room clock—5:34. Roughly seven minutes had passed since I saw the accident from my bedroom.

I looked about my living room for Harmony and didn't see her. Maybe she was in the kitchen checking for snacks. As I staggered that direction, I heard her voice at my back door, "Goodbye, Miss Lizzy. See you tomorrow." And the door slammed shut.

"No! Wait!" I screamed, and ran after her. Exiting my back door just as Harmony reached her rear stoop, I waved frantically and shouted her name.

With a big smile, she just waved back, then disappeared inside her house.

It was 5:35 on my watch.

Since I couldn't risk trying to catch her through the back, I sped around the side between our houses—intending to head her off at her porch. Now, I'm no longer a spring chicken, as you can easily see. But I could've made it in time if not for that old oak that straddles our property line. In my haste to beat Harmony to her front porch, I tripped on a raised root and went sprawling. Caught a face full of grass and dirt and did something awful to my left wrist. See? It still hurts even six weeks later.

Yes, I'm getting to The Incident. You've been reasonably patient so far... please allow me to finish it properly.

Where was I? Oh, on the ground. I must've lost nearly two minutes getting back to my feet and scrambling to the front edge of the Canada house. So it was about 5:37 by then.

Harmony was standing on their porch with Natalie in the open front doorway, her hand on the child's shoulder.

"Don't let her go!" I screamed.

"What on earth?" exclaimed Natalie as Harmony broke loose and made for the steps.

"A car! An accident! Smack down the mailbox! Keep her away and warn your husband!" If I hadn't lost that time being blotto and the other couple of minutes pulling myself off the ground, perhaps I could've sat down with Natalie in her front room and calmly explained everything. But as it was, all I could do was clutch Harmony tightly and screech at Natalie to race up the street to intercept her husband.

My watch read 5:38.

"Let go of my daughter!" she said, rushing toward us and trying to yank Harmony from my grasp.

"No. I can't. That car's going to hit your mailbox in about ninety seconds and she can't be anywhere near it. Go warn your husband!"

"What car?" She looked around. "What happened to your face?" She peered closer. "There's blood on your forehead and a big knot. What on earth is going on?"

"Natalie, I swear I'll answer all your questions later, but right now you move your butt and catch Tyrell before he gets near that mailbox. There's a light blue muscle car heading this way and it loses control on that curve and hill. Smacks right into your mailbox."

"If you don't release my daughter this instant, I'm calling the police."

"Call them! Call the National Guard. But first, go warn your husband. Listen! Do you hear the tires squealing?"

"I don't hear..."

"If I was half my age, I'd run out there and warn him myself! I've got Harmony. You go get Tyrell."

I could tell by the way she turned her head that she finally heard the roaring engine and squealing tires. The panic in her eyes said more than thousands of words. Natalie jumped off that porch like an Olympic steeplechase runner. Screaming the whole way and waving her arms wildly, she covered her front yard and half of the westerly neighbor's and reached Tyrell, just as the light blue late sixties muscle car passed them, out of control. Fortunately, Tyrell had slowed his regu-

135

lar stride—though not halted entirely—so he was perhaps twenty or thirty seconds off that normal pace which gave him such punctual pride.

Knowing that Harmony was safe on the porch with me and Tyrell was hearing the initial explanation from Natalie, some sixty feet away from the mailbox, I had to close my eyes. I couldn't watch that collision a second time.

But the noise and screams were horrific.

It was 5:40.

Smoke and steam. The car and the mailbox were mangled and tangled—the driver badly injured.

And I guess that's basically it—my whole story. Some have told me that my bedroom clock saved the lives of Harmony and her dad six weeks ago. I guess that's one way of looking at it. I've even had one person tell me it wasn't about the clock at all—rather some strange inter-dimensional shift in the time continuum of that specific room. Me? I don't pretend to know.

Natalie and Tyrell must've thanked me a hundred times for halting him and securing Harmony. Natalie readily and frequently told anyone who'd listen that I'd informed her of the accident in advance, down to the color and type and exact path of the vehicle. Not many believed her, of course.

You seem far less skeptical than most I've spoken to, but if you're not completely convinced, just ask Natalie.

No, I haven't tried moving that clock into a different room. Tell you the truth, I'm a little bit scared of it. I'm of a mind to just leave it be until it stops running, or until I do. I've calculated that if it continues to gain some nine minutes a week, by the end of a complete year, I'll be able to see nearly eight hours into the future. Who knows? Might be useful to know what's going to happen in this neighborhood with that much advance notice.

Their schedule will change once school starts, but since the day of The Incident, Natalie sometimes comes over with Harmony and joins us for tea. She's never asked to go into my bedroom and look out those two windows, but there was a time she mentioned—a bit too casually for it to actually *be* casual—"Anything special happening today?"

How much future can I see right now? I keep a tally right here by my chair—adding about nine minutes per week, it'd be roughly 63 minutes.

I can see you're perplexed. But are you ready to look more than an hour into the future? Anything you can see from either of those bedroom windows. Not sure? Well, think about it. I haven't let anyone else who tried to interview me. But for you, the invitation might remain open.

Oh, and before you turn off that tape machine, make note of this: if I've established one thing in this entire study—whether the clock or the room is the actual cause—it's that you *can* change the future. The question becomes: *should* you change it?

END

That ASMR Girl

Charles A. Salter

FBI DEPUTY DIRECTOR Baker looked perplexed. "The basic facts are these: Colonel Robert Miller, commander of Fort Olson in Maryland, was found dead in his office by the incoming staff duty officer at exactly 0600 hours three days ago. The door and all windows were locked from the inside. No sign of forced entry or violence. Just stiff as a statue, still sitting in his full uniform upright in the chair."

Special Agent Debuey seemed puzzled. "Well, a full bird colonel has got to be up there in years, right? Lots of stress as a base commander. Pulling an all-nighter. Heart attack? Pulmonary embolism? Maybe a stroke?"

Baker looked straight into the other man's piercing eyes. "Negative on that. We're still waiting for the autopsy results to be sure, but he was seemingly in perfect health for his age. The thing which makes this case curious to our superiors is what he had on his desktop computer when he died."

"Ah, so he was warming his willie to internet porn?"

"Negative on that, too, Agent Debuey. The man was fully clothed, all zipped up, but yet with an odd expression on his face... eyes still open and frozen, staring into the computer."

"So what was on the screen?"

"ASMR."

"What the H is that? Never heard of it."

"They'll brief you when you get there. It's only about an hour's drive from here. If you leave now, you can beat the traffic."

"Wait a minute. Why me? Why the FBI? This was on an Army base. Why isn't the CID investigating?"

"That's where this case gets really screwy. The CID *did* look into it."

"So why do they want us?"

"Because two days after Colonel Miller bought the big burrito, the CID agent investigating died also, in exactly the same manner. He was found in his BOQ room on base watching the same ASMR video as Miller."

Debuey felt goosebumps.

"The Assistant SecDef for Homeland Defense personally asked our director to pick up the investigation where the CID left off."

"Yes, sir," said Debuey. "I'm on my way." *And I'm too close to retirement for this crap.*

⟜

THE GUARD AT THE Fort Olson gate took a close look at Debuey's ID, then returned it through his open auto window. "FBI, huh? You must be here to investigate those two deaths on base."

"I'm not allowed to say either way. But do you know anything about them?"

"The whole base is talking about how Miller must have been whacking his mole when he did the dirt dive, in his own office, for Pete's sake. His wife has been out of town for over a month. Went to Florida to help out with some sick grandkids or something."

"How about the second victim, that CID fellow?"

"Don't know much about him. He kept to himself and never went out... never socialized. You know, a classic loner type."

"Thanks." Debuey drove on through to the headquarters in Building 810, where an MP escorted him to the security office.

"Ahh, Special Agent Debuey? Pleased to meet you." A youngish officer in his dress green uniform reached out a hand.

Debuey took it and shook hands but didn't smile. He was feeling tired and old and wished he was past all this, out on his sailboat in the Chesapeake Bay rather than getting involved in what might become the biggest case of his career. Promotions and pay raises no longer interested him. He longed only for rest, for an end to the eternal schedule of rising, commuting, working, commuting, and lying in bed tossing and turning, trying uselessly to sleep before another cycle of stress and fatigue started all over again.

"I'm Captain Tapper, the security watch commander," the man said, breaking off the handshake. "Where would you like to begin?"

"With how the SDO found the colonel Monday morning."

"Would you like to interview the SDO personally?"

"Maybe later. Let's start with your overview."

"The incoming SDO relieved the outgoing, who informed him that Colonel Miller had been in his office all night. Both knocked on his door to make their daily report, but he failed to respond. Finding the door locked, they called in the overnight security watch commander to bring the master key and open the door. That's when they found him."

"So three people entered at the same time and all saw him more or less at once?"

"Affirmative."

"Do their signed statements match up, or were there any discrepancies?"

"No discrepancies in the basic facts as I just outlined. But there were differences in perspective as to what each saw on entry."

"What do you mean?"

"Well, all three agreed that they saw the commander fully dressed, sitting upright at his desk, facing his desktop computer."

"So what was different?"

"The outgoing SDO said Miller looked tired, as if he had gone to sleep with his eyes still open from sheer exhaustion."

"And the incoming SDO?"

"Lieutenant Brubaker has something of a medical background, and he thought perhaps Miller had experienced an aneurism, passing out before he could even blink."

"And the third—the security man?"

"Woman. A Lieutenant Cynthia Lance."

"What did she think?"

"She thought Miller looked radiant, as if he had found nirvana. She stated he had the most ecstatic look on his face she had ever seen in a dead person."

"She has lots of experience with dead people?"

140

"I dunno. Do you want to interview her?"

"Yeah. Let's start with Lieutenant Lance."

∽

WITH THE THREE OF them seated in Capt. Tapper's office, Debuey opened with, "Lieutenant Lance, I'm going to record this interview, okay?"

She nodded.

Debuey pressed a button on his pocket recorder and set it on the table between them. "Let's start with what you saw in Colonel Miller's expression when you first set eyes on him after opening the door. I don't mean his physical position—that's been well established. But your interpretation of his facial expression... maybe some indication of what you think he was thinking or feeling when he died."

"I am a Buddhist by adopted faith, and it appeared to me that Miller had experienced nirvana—the ultimate spiritual release, the highest and most perfect state of human consciousness. Think of a candle, burning bright, then—"

"I'm familiar with the concept of nirvana, Lieutenant. But why do you say Colonel Miller experienced it? Was he a Buddhist, too?"

"Not so far as I know. He never attended any of our meetings."

"So why do you apply that term to him?"

"Because I thought his face shone with perfect bliss and contentment."

"Compared to what?"

"Compared to all the other recent dead I have seen."

"You deal with a lot of dead people?"

"I wouldn't say deal. I attend countless wakes and funerals and memorial services and the like, not only for fellow members of our group, but neighbors, work friends, everyone I know."

What an odd pre-occupation. "Did you by any chance also see the body of that CID agent investigating Miller's death?"

"I did. I was on duty that night also and was called in immediately when the maid at the BOQ found his body."

"Do you have any thoughts about *his* facial expression?"

"Absolutely. He had found nirvana, too. Only, he was a late-comer."

"What does that mean?"

"Some seek bliss all their lives, while others stumble upon it only at the end, after never seeking it consciously. Those late-comers always have a hint of surprise on their faces as well as the joy."

"Any other similarities or notable differences between these two victims?"

"Both were alone at the time of their deaths, so no eyewitnesses. But both were military men in good physical shape despite being in late middle age. I wasn't assigned to investigate, so that's about all I know. The CID man had been on base for years, but I never really knew him. I'd see him once in a while at staff meetings, and that was about it."

"Thank you, Lieutenant Lance. That will be all for now."

She stood and left the room, shutting the door behind her.

Debuey turned to the captain. "Did you detect any other similarities or notable differences between the two victims?"

"Well, I second what Lieutenant Lance just said. I would never see CID Special Agent Grimes except at staff meetings when he filled in for his boss, which wasn't often. And out running on the PT track or working out in the gym."

"Married?"

"Negative. He had been married when younger. But he was a widower for something like ten or twelve years at least. So he lived alone. No family in the region, though I think he had some relatives out on the west coast whom he rarely saw. He kept to himself mostly. A classic loner."

Just like me. "So no sign of breaking and entering by an outside party? Completely alone in his BOQ as far as we know?"

"As far as we know. And I checked the elevator and hallway surveillance tapes. He went to his room right after work. A couple of hours later, he had a pizza delivery service send up dinner. That was his only outside contact until the maid found his body the next morning."

"Do we need to interview the pizza guy?"

"I already did. And I saw the whole encounter on the vids. About sixty seconds in duration, and the pizza guy never entered the room. He stood there in the hall, handed over the pizza, grabbed his money, and left. Seemed unhappy with the small tip, but by the time his face turned sour, Agent Grimes had already shut the door and was alone again."

"Speaking of vids, do you have any idea what Miller was looking at on the computer when he achieved this so-called nirvana?"

"I've never heard of it before, but I understand it was something called ASMR."

"What *is* that, anyway?"

"Why don't you interview the forensic psychologist assigned to this case next? She can explain."

AN ATTRACTIVE BRUNETTE civilian wearing a white blouse and blue skirt entered the door.

Debuey at once felt a tingle in the back of his head. *She is luscious.* He smiled, rose to his feet, and greeted her. "Pleased to meet you, Dr.—"

"Ainsworth. Maxeala Ainsworth. Most of my colleagues call me Max." She didn't smile back, but stiffly shook his hand.

He noticed her professional coolness, and his smile dropped. "Well, since we've just met, I'll stick with Dr. Ainsworth."

"As you wish. What can I help you with?"

"You've been looking into the Miller case?"

"Yes. They wanted me to do a psychological profile on the man... a psychological autopsy, if you will. Particularly whether we could rule out suicide or not."

"And have you made that determination yet?"

"Not a final one. I still haven't had a chance to interview the widow yet. She rushed back from her trip, of course, to face this situation, but she's been so busy with funeral details that I didn't want to intrude. But I have completed every other aspect of my investigation and so far found no indication whatsoever of suicide."

"And you've been looking also into the other case—that CID agent?"

She nodded.

"From what I've been told, both cases have something to do with ASMR."

"That is correct."

"I'm not exactly certain what ASMR even is. Could you explain it in layman's terms, please?"

"Of course. It is an acronym standing for autonomous sensory meridian response."

"But what does that *mean?*"

"Well, if you look at each of the four words separately, then add their meanings together, I would put it like this—an autonomous, or independently generated, peak—or meridian—emotional response to certain sensory stimuli."

"You've still got me scratching my chin. What kind of stimuli?"

"Practitioners of ASMR typically use videos that present various stimuli meant to relax viewers and help them fall asleep. Things like smiling, speaking in soft whispers, saying upbeat and supportive phrases, tapping on bottles of lotion, rhythmically swaying their hands and fluttering their fingers, making lip-smacking or kissing noises..."

"Kissing... you mean like in online porn?"

"Not at all. Some pornographers have attempted to add ASMR triggers to their product, but almost no viewers care much for that. Porno fans say the soft and gentle ASMR triggers detract from the arousal of the porn, while ASMR connoisseurs complain that nudity or overt sexuality of any kind ruins the pure ASMR effect."

"I'm not sure I fully understand. Arousal is arousal, right? Stimulus and response."

"But, you see, unsullied ASMR reaches deeper into the psyche than sex. It goes for a more primal level than sex. Genital stimulation has nothing to do with it."

"You gotta give me some more. What is more primal than sex?"

"What are *your* first memories, Special Agent Debuey?"

"I dunno. Being age three or four, maybe. Playing on the floor at home. Hugging the dog. Seeing my mother."

"Any sex in those earliest memories?"

He choked back a laugh. "Of course not."

"So that stage of life is more primal than sex, and that is just your first conscious memories. Go back even further, further to a time before conscious thought, back to infancy. Back to being four or six *months* old, things your conscious mind can't remember at all, but your unconscious clings to still."

"My unconscious remembers *what?*"

"Being at peace. Being loved. Having your mother bend over you in the crib and take care of you, cooing, cleaning, wiping away your tears."

"So these videos are of mothers tending to children?"

"Not consciously. But the most popular ones have iconically beautiful women who seem to adore you, who zoom in close to their cameras to show their loving eyes and sweet expressions, who open and close boxes of wet wipes or shake bottles of baby oil."

"Giving the conscious experience of simply presenting positive stimuli or triggers?"

"Now you're getting it," continued Dr. Ainsworth. "No one but a psychologist would link all this back to early infancy, but if you look at the most popular triggers, they are mostly things a newborn would experience while looking up at a loving mother."

"So no sex. No porn."

"Of course not. ASMR devotees note no genital stimulation. Scientific studies of their brains while viewing ASMR, measuring brain response with CT scans or PET scans, reveal little to no activation of the sexual regions in the brain, but rather what I call colloquially the bliss center. No point in me naming the exact brain structures since I doubt you've studied neuroanatomy."

He shook his head. "But what you are describing sounds to me wholesome and positive. So how can these responses be dangerous? Didn't they kill two men on this base just this week?"

Capt. Tapper broke in. "Let me remind you that we don't know the precise cause of death, nor how these men died."

Debuey looked at the captain. "Good point. Thank you."

Looking back at Dr. Ainsworth, he continued, "So is it possible for ASMR to be dangerous?"

"Is dihydrogen oxide dangerous? Should we ban that because some people don't get enough and die of deprivation, while others get too much and die of intoxication? While others fall into such a large quantity that they die from being unable to breathe?"

"I know that old internet joke, Doctor. Dihydrogen oxide is H-two-O, simply pure water. Thirst can kill, drinking too much can kill, and you can drown."

She chuckled. "Most things in life are both essential and dangerous. You must strive for a balance in all things."

"So is it possible to lose one's 'balance' with ASMR?"

"I wouldn't have thought so. Research studies have never reported that before. Something like twenty to thirty per cent of people viewing an ASMR video for the first time wonder what all the fuss is about. It does nothing for them. Another third or so of people get tingles right off the bat, a kind of thrill starting in their spines or the back of their heads and shivering itself up and down through their whole bodies, leaving them feeling satisfied, relaxed, and content."

"And the rest?"

"If they are interested enough to keep trying, if they really need help relaxing, feeling peaceful, and falling asleep, they can watch a number of different videos by different artists, and keep sampling 'til they find the triggers that work for them."

"I see. And what was apparently working for Colonel Miller and the CID man?"

"An artist who has called herself differing names over time. I think it was originally 'ASMR-pure-angel' or something like that, but then lots of artists started working the term angel into their online handles."

"Why?"

"As I said, the best ASMR is not sexual, so angel helps promote the image that these performances are pure and spiritual, the performers standing in for universal archetypes of the essence of femininity but on such a high plane that one can behold their beauty but not even think of debasing them with carnal thoughts or feelings."

"Well, I don't see how anything that noble could possibly lead to someone's death."

"Maybe it didn't. Remember, we don't know yet."

"I have a theory," broke in Capt. Tapper.

"Yes?" encouraged Debuey.

"Although I had never even heard of ASMR before, I had a quick glance at the one Colonel Miller was watching. It was the most gorgeous woman I had ever seen in any media form in my entire life. It seemed she was my world, my universe, beckoning me to join her in perfect bliss. It reminded me of the legend of Odysseus and his voyage in Homer's epic poem, the part where the supernatural sirens' enchanting voices compelled sailors to steer a course towards them. I can imagine forgetting even to breathe in the presence of something that powerful—"

Debuey noted Tapper blanched, abruptly stopped speaking, and glanced nervously at the psychologist, as if he realized he had shared more than he should have in front of an on-base colleague. Debuey intervened and turned towards the psychologist. "Forgetting even to breathe. What do you make of that, Dr. Ainsworth?"

"Well, as I said, there is nothing in the medical literature about that. All the scientific research suggests some people don't respond at all, while many others find it peaceful and relaxing, a non-drug aid to sleep. But as I also said, without balance in one's life, maybe too much could become a problem for a tiny minority of people. I would guess less than one per cent of the population, if that. Someone older, isolated, more lonely might get so wrapped up that he would forget to take care of himself... maybe ignore bodily signals like cardiac pain or dizziness, failing to notice a heart attack or something like that until it was too late. Until the final autopsy report comes in, we won't know for sure exactly how these two men died."

Old, isolated, lonely—you've just described me. "Wait a second, Dr. Ainsworth. We keep talking about men looking at feminine angels in these videos. Don't they make ASMR for women, too? Don't women respond?"

"Well if you go back to my theory about early infancy and unconscious, deeply primal experiences, of course girls respond to their mothers also, but not in the same way as most little boys. And as adults, females can and do react with relaxation to videos of female artists performing ASMR. But there are also male artists who perform ASMR specifically aimed at women, most of whom no doubt had warm and close relationships with their fathers from a young age."

"So again, nothing sexual. This is not parallel to a woman getting excited by reading racy romance books?"

"Absolutely correct."

"But male-produced ASMR wasn't involved here," Debuey continued, "so let's drop that line of thought."

"Of course."

"Could you show me a specific clip of the female-produced video that may—or may not—have had something to do with two male deaths on base this week?"

Dr. Ainsworth pulled out her smartphone. "Certainly. The sound and visuals on this tiny screen don't give you quite the full experience, but should give you some sense of what they were watching." She fiddled with a few buttons and then laid the phone on the table and slid it close enough for him to see.

Capt. Tapper also looked over. "That's the one, all right. She really is an angel."

Debuey was instantly mesmerized. The most beautiful woman he had ever seen. A musical voice like in the greatest opera ever filmed. She leaned in close to two microphones positioned as if on a human head, with each in the corresponding spot for an ear, one to the left, the other to the right. *The camera must be directly above the mics*, he thought. She whispered in one 'ear' then the other. The mics were so ultrasensitive that he could almost hear her eyelids blink. As her hands moved and fingers fluttered they made the sounds of holy doves descending from the heavens. The lip and tongue sounds were magical and entrancing, every breath deeply intoxicating.

Thrill after thrill tingled up the back of his scalp and exploded out of his head with a shiver. He felt peaceful, relaxed, at one with the universe.

Move over, Odysseus. I could also forget to breathe while watching this, he thought.

He checked himself, not wanting either colleague to note that he was experiencing a bit of nirvana also, right out in public.

Debuey glanced at the clock on the wall. "It's getting late. Thank you, Dr. Ainsworth, for your time. I expect to be here about a week or so. If I have any further questions, I'll let you know." He turned to the captain. "Where am I spending the night?"

"I have you booked into the on-base BOQ. It's relatively new and very nice. I think you'll find it agreeable."

Debuey smiled dreamily, still relaxed from his first taste of ASMR. *Can't wait to get to my room and explore this amazing vid further...*

IN LANGLEY, VIRGINIA, Agent Radisson was arguing with her boss. "Wait a minute. Why me? Why the CIA? This was on an Army base. Why isn't the CID investigating?"

"That's where this case gets really screwy. The CID *did* look into it."

"So why do they want us?"

"Because there may be counter-terrorism issues involved. Two days after Colonel Miller waved his final sayonara, the CID agent investigating died also... in exactly the same manner. He was found in his BOQ room on base watching the same ASMR video as Miller. Ditto a couple of days later for the FBI special agent—something Debuey—doing the follow-up investigation."

Radisson felt goosebumps. "So why me?"

"There's something about the women in these videos which may have killed three senior government officials—all men. The director thought that you, being... ah... a woman might be more immune."

I must hide it pretty well, thought Radisson. *Do they really not know that I prefer girls, too?*

Later that night in her room at the on-base bachelor officers' quarters, she turned on her laptop to update her evidence notes and check out for herself what the fuss was all about.

She fed in the URL and up popped an amazing display.

Ummm, umm, mmm, she thought. What a perfect angel. It would be worth it to stop breathing for her...

END

Blade of Grass

J. L. Salter

Late April, 2026

I'D SPENT MORE TIME on our cabin's front porch that day because Rover was acting like he'd heard something in the woods. Or smelled it. Or maybe that old pooch just sensed something. Anyway, I'd rolled out to the porch and watched, my binoculars nearby on the weathered railing. Otherwise, it was a morning like most others in rural Kentucky's late April.

"You expecting someone, Grandpa?" asked Jessica, my older granddaughter, as she bounded up the steps briefly between her various outdoor chores. She was sixteen, more of a tomboy than a young lady—strong, toned, tanned, and used to hard work. My wife and I had been raising Jessica and her younger sister for the past three and a half years.

"Not sure," I said, tugging closed the front of my jacket against the cool breeze. "But Rover sure is acting funny."

"Maybe it'll be another person who needs help. What was it Grandma called them?"

"Panhandler," I replied, "but that has a connotation of a beggar. Most of these folks aren't beggars." I closed my eyes for a second to think. "When my parents were young, the term would've been hobo or tramp."

"Tramp?" The word puzzled her.

"It meant something different back then. Basically just meant they were homeless, on the road, and on foot. Looking for a place to lay their heads where they'd be reasonably protected from the elements and safe from..."

"Violence?"

I nodded.

"So who do you think it'll be this time?"

"A lone traveler, I hope. Someone we can give water from the spring and send on their way with a sandwich... or more, if your grandma has something ready."

"We've had quite a few come by here. You ever think about counting them, Grandpa?"

"Not any point. Besides, it wouldn't be right to keep a tally of good deeds done." I flicked at a bug that had landed on my heavily-veined hand. "We put something in their bellies and send them on with our blessing."

"You've let some of them stay a night or two in the barn. I remember one had a fever and Grandma nursed him out of it." Jessica thought for a moment. "And one man had a broken arm that you set—he stayed here several days, I think."

"True, and there have been others," I replied, "but we have to be careful. Some might not be folks we can trust to settle for what we give them and not simply take what they want."

"How can you tell the difference, Grandpa?"

"You can't always. But I'm pretty good at figuring out who's become a victim to the desperate circumstances of our time, and which ones are actually despicable people victimizing others."

"I don't see how you can tell from just meeting them."

"It's partly to do with their attitudes," I said, still scanning the fields to our east. "The ones who've fallen into desperate circumstances are more typically relying on themselves, but will gladly accept a bit of assistance. The others likely come here looking for what they can take and figure they have as much right to what they see as the person who owns it. Sort of like bullies at school, if you can remember back that far."

Her nod signaled a memory as she gazed down the curving three-mile stretch of dirt and gravel that we called our driveway in this rather isolated section of Poldark County. "Not sure I yet understand how you can tell the difference without knowing them for a while."

"One way has to do with weapons. Lots of travelers are armed these days, of course, but the ones I'm more inclined to trust—and try to help—are those who carry their guns like tools. You know, they keep their guns stowed out of sight and don't make any moves to retrieve them. And—as you've probably noticed—when they arrive, one of our first discussions involves the proper storage of their firearms while they're here."

"The others?"

"The others are usually armed to the teeth, have their guns pointed *at* us as they approach... and their firearms represent leverage. They also seem to figure their weapons give them some special *right* to take what they want and do what they wish with the actual residents."

She shuddered. "Wish we could tell before they get close."

"That's part of the reason for these glasses," I said, pointing to the binoculars.

Jessica's eyes followed the line of my gaze. She and her sister had been through a lot, losing their parents so suddenly. Linda and I had done our best, but in addition to grief at the loss of our son, we'd suffered our own problems—age and infirmity being the two that affected nearly everything else. I knew Jessica and Sissy needed proper schooling, but that was impossible in our circumstances. Not to mention that it was far too dangerous for them, these days.

"You remember my friend over at the next farm?" she asked rhetorically.

Of course I knew the Fensters. Our long-time neighbors, about seven miles up the county road. Quite a bit younger than Linda and me, and they had a son between the ages of our two granddaughters. To Jessica, I silently nodded.

"Well, Dick told me last week that he'd heard his dad talking about a group of armed men that had come into Grahamville and caused a lot of trouble."

I'd heard about that—the little town was some twenty miles away. "Honey, you know towns are better targets for troublemakers." I did my best to comfort her. "We're three miles from that county road over yonder and it goes to a dead-end, up past the Fensters' farm. No reason for anybody to be on that road unless they live out this way. Plus it doesn't connect to the nearest highway for at least eight miles the other direction."

Both girls had been driving my ancient tractor (with a wide-cut belly mower) since they'd arrived here. Sissy was not even ten at that point. I'd waited 'til she was twelve to teach her the operation of the backhoe with the scoop up front. Jessica, however, had taken to both almost from her first month here and also quickly mastered the dozer with interchangeable grader blade and loader bucket.

"Well, let us know if you and Rover spot anybody, so we can get things ready." At that, Jessica went back inside.

I'd used this chair since my leg pain became too rough for crutches to be my primary mode—some eighteen months now. At age 83, I could still hobble about on the sticks, but I wasn't much use as far as chores and such. When the pain hit harder than usual—when the weather changed dramatically, for example—I'd catch myself rubbing one knee after the other. In doing so, it made a little ripple, with what remained of my forearm muscles, under my tattoo of the 7th Cavalry Division. That was long ago, however. Different time, and me a different man. Back then I was a young buck, tall and straight, strong enough to carry my own load and more. Sometimes that memory was as thin and faded as this old tattoo. *Days long gone.*

Last time Linda and I had been to town was for the presidential election in November 2024. That short trip had represented the final journey of my old pickup truck.

My wife used to do lots of things like sewing, needlepoint, and other crafts. The last piece she did before her eyes got so bad had been a needlework gift for me—a rustic field scene with the legend "Blade of Grass." Linda could still manage around the kitchen, I guess because the layout was so familiar, but it was too dangerous for her to go outside much, especially not by herself. I hadn't verbalized this to anyone, but I reckoned Linda and I were dependent on the two girls at least as much as they relied upon us.

It was easy enough to see that sixteen-year-old Jessica wanted more of a life than could be had on this isolated farm, and I figured a time might come when she'd want to break away. So I did everything in my power to make her feel comfortable here and not over-burdened with the chores I could no longer do. Of course, that meant a lot of things had fallen into disrepair.

I used to have a good friend, Waylon, who'd stop by now and then and help with things—that was back before we got the girls here. But my somewhat younger friend left his modest rented farm when the bank took it back, and he went to Louisville looking for work. These four long years, I never heard from him again (and it was a while before I learned why). But then the mail hardly ran to the rural areas any more, due to the government cutbacks. And in the larger cities it had become too dangerous for the delivery people—too many were dragged from their vehicles and, if they were lucky, just beat up real bad. The vehicle stolen, of course. Sometimes I wondered where all that mail was piling up, but it was just one puzzlement among a barrel full that I'd never solve. I didn't have any bills to speak of, anyway. We owned the farm outright. Our water—modern enough indoor plumbing, thank you very much—came from two sources, a spring and a well. We had sufficient varied livestock to keep meat, milk, and eggs on the table. For heat and cooking, we burned wood and I'd stored more cords of cut wood than could be counted. These days, one had to stockpile what was important. What little electric power we used came from a sizeable solar panel my son had installed for us when the girls were still small. Hank Junior had also rigged a solar water heater system, so we had enough hot water for dishes and bathing.

Rover perked up his ears again, but didn't move his head. That couldn't be anything important or he'd rise up and sniff.

I worried about what might happen to the girls after Linda and I passed on, or became so additionally infirm that we'd wish we had. I knew Jessica would take care of Sissy because the older sibling took after her dad. Like our son, Jessica was quick to learn, dependable, responsible, and mature beyond her years. Hank Junior and his wife Maura had tried to stay in the big city after the midterm elections of November 2022, and they were killed in the wide-spread rioting over those next several weeks. These three and a half years, they've laid in rest under the shade of that 200-year old oak on the south side of our cabin, not too far from the run-down barn. I'd never mentioned this to anybody, not even my wife, but I'd noticed although Jessica often passed by those graves and usually stopped for a moment of reflection or respect, I'd never seen Sissy go near that site.

I GUESS I MIGHT well have dozed off on the porch that fair mid-morning, if not for Rover's head jerking up and him giving a low, steady growl as he immediately gained his feet and stood next to my chair.

"What do you see, boy?" I asked as I scanned with my field glasses. "Animal or human?" At times like this, I wished Rover used human words, though he likely believed he'd told me what I needed to know. *Something approaches that doesn't belong here.* At least I knew exactly where it was. Rover was visually focused on the curve in our three-mile drive.

I didn't yet see anything or anyone, but I knew it would be only moments before whatever Rover had detected finally made that curve and became visible to us at the cabin. Shivering a bit, I called into the cabin, "Jessica, I feel a chill coming on. Would you fetch my special blanket from the magazine room?"

Though she didn't reply, I could hear her movements and quickly she appeared. "Somebody coming?"

"So says Rover." I arranged the blanket over my lap, with the long side to my right... taking care that it not get tangled in either wheel.

Shortly, there he was. A lone human. Male.

Travelers by themselves were often just other innocent citizens like myself—in hard times, trying to make do. Unlike me, who had a place and was rooted to it by infirmity, they wandered, always hoping to find better circumstances. This one *could* be a hobo or a tramp, but through the 8X magnification of my binoculars, I didn't get the sense of a dejected man who'd been on the road for months or years. This thin, medium-height male was younger than I'd expect in a typical tramp... and as I just now detected, he held a fancied-up black rifle.

After those congressional midterms of November 2022, firearms registries had been retrieved from databases which federal agencies had long sworn were never collected nor retained. People like me had known all along that such information *was* being compiled and it was only a matter of time before it was put to use, like they'd done decades before in Australia and Great Britain. The first national round-ups had begun nearly immediately after the January 2025 inauguration of America's first openly socialist president. In the celebratory rush of those first hundred days, the new chief executive and her hastily assembled new cabinet had crammed through legislation making all privately owned firearms illegal and thereby—overnight—turning millions of law-abiding citizens into *de facto* felons. Many, like my buddy Waylon, were arrested when they were found with a gun. In his case, by the Louisville police, an antique double-barreled 12-gauge shotgun he'd inherited from his grandfather. Afterwards, I'd no longer seen or heard from Waylon.

During the same time Hank and Maura were killed, many of the larger—already depressed—industrial-based cities had rapidly become war zones. With the resulting exodus of people hoping to live in peace, the criminals also had to branch out from those urban centers to find replacement targets. Like the so-called army ants of South America, they radiated out in all directions, destroying everything as they went.

The initial effects in rural areas, like ours, was the drying up of the supply lines—the trucking of groceries and fuel had abruptly ceased. No newspapers were delivered any more. Only later did the raiding bands begin to terrorize rural areas, but it was haphazard. City criminals understood how to "harvest" a grocery store, but they were clueless about acquiring food from the land where it grew.

When the hair on Rover's back bristled, I looked again through the glasses and hoped I would see the lone traveler sling his rifle, which would've hinted that his intentions were peaceful. Instead, this man—evidently because he'd finally spotted me on my porch—eased his black shoulder gun around... pointing directly at our cabin.

Still, the verdict was out—he *could* be just an innocent traveler seeking assistance, but merely lacking in manners and proper firearm safety protocol. Between Rover and me, however, we'd pretty much concluded this individual was up to no good. As the stranger slowly made his way toward our cabin, I could discern his rifle looked to be a variant of the once quite popular —but now at the top of the banned list— AR-15 platform. Otherwise innocent citizens caught with guns in that configuration were automatically slapped with doubled sentences, as per the new federal dictates.

When he got closer still, it was clear to see the stranger also had a holstered semi-auto pistol on his belt. Was it still possible he was friendly? Sure. But not likely. I already had him figured as an advance scout for some number of others much like him.

The stranger covered the remaining portion of my driveway relatively quickly and soon was standing about sixty yards from my front porch.

"That's far enough," I yelled. "No need to come any closer. If you come in peace, you're welcome to get a drink at our spring and we can spare you a bite to eat. Otherwise, there's nothing here for you."

The scout kept coming, his rifle still aimed generally toward me and the porch.

"I said, that's far enough." I swept my hand left and right. "My property is posted. You'd better leave now."

Not yet having spoken, the stranger continued his strides and finally paused about twenty-five feet from my front steps, from where he scrutinized me and the cabin. If he'd been cleaned up and appropriately dressed, he might have been presentable—looked to be mid-twenties, though age was difficult to calculate with such folks.

"I'm going to ask you politely to point that rifle somewhere else, pilgrim."

The scout considered my request and then shrugged. "Well, mister, since you asked so nice and all." He veered his barrel off to the right, almost as level as a transit shift, but—unwisely and dangerously—kept his finger on the trigger.

"Nothing here to interest you. I'm a lonely old man in the middle of nowhere with barely enough to live on. Leave me be."

"You ain't alone out here, old man," stated the stranger. "I've been watching from the woods."

That finally explained what had concerned Rover earlier. "Nothing here for you. You're trespassing."

"Our boss said the private property laws don't matter no more," replied the scout. "Finally, everything belongs to everybody."

I was shaking my head. "This place is mine, bought and paid for, long before you were born. Tell your boss to move along. It was a thriving farm in its time, but nothing here now except briars, weeds, and uncut grass."

"And maybe a few, um, valuables hidden in all that unmowed field."

"Nothing here that would benefit you."

"Maybe so, maybe not." He took another look at the cabin, barn, and chicken yard. "Okay, I'm going... but I'll be back." Then he turned. "And next time, I won't be alone."

As I figured. I watched as the scout trudged back down my graveled dirt drive. Later, I made a final check with my binoculars as he rounded the curve, about halfway. It took him nearly twenty minutes to make it that far.

Jessica opened the front door just a crack and whispered from inside. "Okay to come out?"

"Yeah. He's around the curve now." Plus he'd already seen either her or Sissy as he'd secretly reconnoitered my farm earlier.

"You think he'll come back?"

Undoubtedly. I just nodded. "Get your sister from the kitchen and you two move all the livestock into the barn. Batten down the shutters of the hen house. Bring Rover inside and lock him in the magazine room. Close all the window shutters and latch them tight, except that small window on the side. Tell your grandma that pretty soon I figure we'll probably have some more company."

IT WAS NEARLY THREE hours later that the armed scout reappeared around the curve of our drive, and at least another twenty minutes before he reached the cabin. Not much for me to do but wait in my chair.

As before, he stopped about twenty-five feet from my steps. Again, his black rifle pointed toward me. "I'm back."

"That's a big mistake, pilgrim."

"Well, our boss is intent on meeting you. Plus, like I said before, I've been watching from the woods and I spotted a girl or two. Might be even more women inside somewhere. We'd like to be introduced." He laughed crudely.

"Go back and tell your boss to move along. Nothing here but misery—briars, weeds, and tall grass."

"Yeah, yeah, so you said. But grass don't bother me. All this place needs is one of those tractor things... can't remember what they call it."

"Bushhog."

"Right. Just drive a bushhog around this place and clean it up. No more briars or high grass."

"A vigorous tangle of briars will help keep away certain varmints," I said calmly. "And I like the blades of good, healthy grass... they give me comfort in my old age." I watched him for a reaction, but saw none. "Plus, my bushhog is busted, like everything else around here. Now move on."

"Too late, old man. My boss is right behind me... with a few of our friends."

I could finally see them, just coming around the curve. Moving slowly and all clumped together—one sixteen-ounce M-26 Lemon grenade would've taken out all six of them. I reckoned they'd arrive in about fifteen minutes or so. "Still plenty of time for you to jog back and tell your boss and friends to move along. Nothing here for you but misery."

"That little speech about grass is getting pretty old. You need some new material. I also seen those two girls. Boss thinks maybe there's more than two."

"Go back down the county road to the highway," I said, pointing toward the party approaching behind him. "Last warning."

"No problem, old man," replied the scout. "My job is to hold you here on the porch 'til my buddies arrive." He shifted his weight from foot to foot several times over those slow fifteen minutes.

Meanwhile, I eased my chair over a bit, so I had a clearer view of the area in front of my porch.

Finally the boss appeared with his other five thugs—all heavily armed, and each had at least one weapon aimed at my cabin. Their leader was squat and thick and decidedly ugly, wearing a suspender and belt rig from the era of Desert Storm, which I figured he'd stolen somewhere. He had a rifle of the Russian AK-47 type, along with two visible handguns of indeterminate caliber or capacity. Besides all that, his belt carried a machete, on whose grip he rested his left hand after he stopped beside his scrawny scout. "So this is the old man who doesn't want no company."

The scout merely nodded. "Claims he lives alone, too."

"We'll soon find out." The one they called Boss removed his ball cap and wiped a sleeve on his forehead before recovering his head. "No name on the mailbox way out there by the road."

"My name is my own business, and I don't think we'll be acquainted long enough for it to matter to you. Meantime, you may address me as *mister* or *lieutenant.*"

The reaction of Boss was an explosive mixture of laughter and coughing. "Look here, Potz," he said to his scout while his eyes kept me fixed, "we got us a lively old coot. A Mister Lieutenant Coot."

Potz grinned appropriately as he slung his AR-15 clone and pulled a semi-auto pistol from a belt holster.

I nodded. "And this is my place."

"Yeah," said Boss. "I already heard that you're hung up on some old-timer notion about private property. Problem is, everything belongs to *the people* now. And we're the people."

I shook my head slowly. "You're a pack of undisciplined animals. And you'd better take off."

Though Boss had started to motion his men to what were likely pre-assigned—and often practiced—activities, my deliberate insult had hit home and he halted them.

"Hold on," he said, a bit louder than was necessary. "We didn't come here to be insulted." There was grumbling agreement from his cadre. "And particularly not from Old Lieutenant Mister Coot."

More agreement and cursing from the others.

"You fellows are making a big mistake here and the irony is that you have no idea how much trouble you're taking on." I paused to let that sink in. "You know, I'm alone now, but my late wife used to teach children and she often told them they always had choices. Right now you still have a choice, which is to leave as fast as you can herd these six ignorant punks who blindly follow you."

When I'd begun speaking, Boss had scowled. Now he grinned with a distinctly un-humorous expression. "You talk pretty big for an old veteran coot, all crippled up. And we just came here to be friendly."

I shook my head. "My farm's in ruins, my truck's broke down. What could I possibly have that would interest you?"

"You got a nice old barn there. Maybe there's a horse I can ride."

"No horse."

"I see a chicken hut. Maybe we'll get us a big omelet."

"Only two chickens left and both stopped laying."

Boss turned to his buddies. "This guy's all hard luck, ain't he? That's a real shame."

"Plenty of good reason for you to move along. Stick to the cities where there's still some food and transportation." I pointed north with a wave of my hand. "Out here, all we have is misery—briars, weeds, and tall blades of grass."

"Yeah, my man Potz told me about your obsession with weeds and grass," said Boss. "I guess all you ignorant farmers are just alike. Hung up with working the land 'til it kills you."

"There's worse ways to die."

After a pause, Boss changed the subject. "I see you got one of them army tattoos, Mister Lieutenant. Which war was you in?"

"Not that it would interest you—and it's none of your business either—but I served during the Vietnam era."

To his buddies, over his shoulder, Boss replied, "Look here, guys, we got us another ancient Nam warrior. Plus he was a giving-out-orders officer. And this one's rolling around in a crummy chair. A wheelchair warrior officer. Ain't you guys skeered?"

Appropriate hoots and chuckles from his band, still clustered together.

Boss obviously enjoyed approbation from his well-traveled audience. "All that irony stuff you were yakking about—the irony's on you, Lieutenant Mister. We've got things to tend to before we leave."

I shifted slightly in my chair. "Since you evidently don't plan to heed my repeated warnings, at least give me some idea of who I'm dealing with. What's your affiliation?"

Another combination of laughter and coughing. "We ain't got no affiliation," replied Boss. Over his shoulder to the guys, he added, "Mister Lieutenant thinks we go to church!"

Appropriate hoots and curses from his gang.

I waited for them to settle back down before I continued. "I meant which gang of thugs and cut-throats are you affiliated with? Crips, Bloods, MS-13, MS-15?"

"We don't pay no dues to nobody, man," he answered. "Don't need somebody else's colors to know what we want and what we're gonna take."

"So you're just freelancers?" I pulled my late uncle's pen knife from my shirt pocket, unfolded the longer blade, and slowly cut a tiny notch into the porch railing nearest my chair.

"Look at this, guys. Our wheelchair warrior lieutenant coot is also a woodworker."

During a lengthy silence, I heard a slight rustle of movement near the small side window in the cabin behind me... but all were secure for the moment behind the heavy, barred door and windows.

It was easy to see this gaggle was impatient to get on with their purposes here—lots of looking around and shifting of feet.

Likely also aware of his band's status, Boss again switched topics. "So you said you went to Nam, huh? Do anything over there besides dump napalm on village babies?"

"Not that you actually care or that it's any of your business, but I was in a little conflict in the Ia Drang valley." I hadn't expected that name to register... and it didn't.

Boss shrugged. "So when was this stupid valley of interest to anybody besides you?"

Briefly I wondered if it was even worth the extra few seconds to educate him, and then replied, "Middle November of 1965. But we're just wasting time here. Move along."

This encounter of the past several minutes had probably gone completely unlike most of the others Boss had undertaken with his band of thugs. He'd lost control of the situation almost from the outset and it was evident he felt a bit defensive. Time, I figured, for him to shift into gear.

"Well, I'm tired of yakking with you, old man," he said, peeking briefly over his shoulder for nods of affirmation. "We're gonna take a look around and see what else you have in this dump that might interest us." Boss motioned for two guys to check the barn. "You three stay here out front," he said pointing to them. "Me and Potz will see who's inside this run-down cabin. Could be lots of goods inside." His rifle aimed toward me, he took a step forward.

"Last warning. Private property. Castle doctrine," I said, discreetly easing my right hand beneath my lap blanket. "I'm legally allowed to use every means at my disposal to prevent vandalism, theft, or invasion of my home."

"No more private anything, man," replied Boss, with what had become a typical sneer. "Where you been, Lieutenant Coot? All that castle crap went out the window last year. It's all about sharing stuff, now. And we're here to share whatever you got. Everything belongs to everybody now, and we're everybody."

"I've given you every conceivable opportunity," I said, my left hand whipping the blanket from my lap. "But now I'm through talking." I quickly pulled my carbine to chest-high firing position.

"Whoa, dude," exclaimed Boss, stepping back reflexively. "You can't have no guns. Ain't you heard? It's against the law now." His eyes and rifle still on me, he addressed his buddies. "We just caught us a major felon, guys. Look at him up in that wheelchair, breaking the law with that little wooden rifle." He stepped to one side and motioned the others forward. "C'mon. We're getting those girls and whatever else is in this shack."

I shot him—twice. Chest, dead center.

As the others ducked reflexively, Boss's poised finger got off a single shot, which struck somewhere on my porch. Then he simply folded to the dirt and gravel with a look on his face of pure astonishment. The .30 caliber carbine bullet doesn't have as much knock-down power as its larger cousin, the .30-06—it won't slam you into next week. But it kills just as good, especially at such short range.

Not quite sure what to do, the other six—crouched or sprawled—kept their guns trained on me and looked anxiously toward the scout. Potz likely already realized he was their newly-appointed spokesman, but it took him a few seconds to figure out how to react. "What is it with you old guys and your antique army rifles?" He appeared to have zero remorse over the abrupt death of their leader.

"Beat it, punk. And drag that carcass with you."

As I had predicted, Potz didn't move. "Where'd you get that little wooden rifle, old man? Didn't you get the word? New law—everybody's gotta turn them in."

"I forgot."

"Very funny," replied the former scout, now leader. Since it was obvious Potz had no idea how to proceed, he resorted to chatter. "So where'd you get that old thing? And how come no uniforms came for it?"

"Why do you care? Are you with the BATFE?"

"The what?"

A few of the five guys behind him had regained their feet and were looking about nervously. This raid had not turned out the way they'd likely imagined. Each still had a weapon aimed at me.

"Never mind. It's none of your business, but I bought it from a friend, who bought it from a friend, who inherited it from his father, back before the government documented every single purchase of guns and ammunition."

My history lesson was lost on the former scout. As had the leader before him, Potz shrugged and shifted the weight on his feet. And looked around quickly to be sure the gang remained with him.

After a silence long enough for a decision to have been made by the thugs, I finally said, "Tell your guys to put down their arms. Or my next shot kills you."

Potz sputtered briefly, but nobody moved or dropped their weapons. Then he said, "We're here for the girls and some food, and maybe you got some money in there. We ain't leaving."

I nodded. "So you don't need that dead punk to be the brains of your outfit?"

With another shrug, Potz said, "He was too bossy, man."

A slight murmur of agreement came from several of his nervous-looking companions.

"You've ignored all my warnings, starting with our initial discussion about four hours ago," I said, slowly. "That's a special kind of stupid."

"You can't call me stupid," replied Potz. "I'm the *new* brains of this outfit." With a sudden yell, he re-aimed his 9mm pistol.

I shot him in the head as his own bullet smacked into my front door, barely missing me. Potz's newly-celebrated brains exploded out the back of his head like scrambled eggs from a blender. Two thugs behind him were splattered. All five remaining guys were apparently in shock as they flattened to the dirt... but still holding their own guns. They knew nothing about anything, except to follow instructions, and now both leaders were dead on the ground.

Motioning with the barrel of my M-1 carbine, I said, "The rest of you haven't caught on yet?"

No replies, but lots of looking around. Nobody knew who would or should emerge as new leader of the diminishing gang. Soon, however, the tall one on my left rose to a crouch and adjusted the aim of his machine pistol. I took him out with two shots to his left upper chest. His finger being on his trigger, he let loose a short spray of bullets, most of which hit the far side of my porch and a few up at the roofline. Apparently he'd had a full automatic.

Three punks down and only now did the remainder began to scatter. The surviving four kept their guns up and fired wildly toward the porch as they scrambled to get away.

As their bullets crashed into the heavy front door and shuttered windows—plus a few kicking up splinters on the porch decking near my chair—all I could do was hunker into the smallest possible target and exterminate them as quickly as I could acquire them in my sights. From the small window, Jessica fired two blasts of 12 gauge from my double-barreled shotgun.

I WATCHED FOR A few minutes to see if anybody was still moving. They weren't. My aim wasn't as good as it used to be, but none of the four had gotten very far. At thirty to forty feet, I could still hit what I needed to. Plus, I still had at least one live round left, maybe two. No telling which ones Jessica's shotgun had hit.

It was then I noticed a different pain in my lower left leg. Something had hit me, but it didn't feel deep. "You can come out now, Jessica," I called out over my shoulder. "And tell your grandma to get things ready to clean a wound."

"Are you shot?" she asked, breaking open the shotgun and extracting the empty shells.

"Might be a splinter from the porch. Might be grazed by a bullet. We'll see when I get inside."

She disappeared long enough to deliver my message and returned. "Are they all gone?"

"All gone."

She counted the bodies. "Seven?"

I nodded as I wheeled my chair around. "You can let Rover out now."

"Okay," she said, then paused. "Grandpa, if they'd put down their guns, would you have let them go?'

I took a second before responding. "Hard to say, honey. If they got away, they'd just come back, and next time it would be double or triple that number. But I also knew they'd never drop their weapons. It's not in their DNA to surrender."

"Seems a shame, all this dying for no reason."

"I gave them every chance in the world."

"I know. It's just…"

"Jessica, this is about our protection and survival. Like we talked about earlier, when someone comes to our cabin and asks for help, we're most likely to help as we're able. But when a band of armed thugs shows up and demands what we have—and threatens our security and our lives—the decision is clear. It's us or them."

"Yeah, I understand, but when will all this end?"

I wished I had an answer. "Not sure, honey. Without law and order and with most of our citizenry disarmed so they can't defend themselves, it may go on for quite a while."

She shrugged. "I guess until the bad guys run out of bullets."

I had no reply to that. I figured there were still enough good folks who had squirreled away guns and ammo, as I had. In fact, I was often reminded of a telling quote attributed to the Japanese Admiral Yamamoto well before their attack on Pearl Harbor, as he'd pointed out the difficulty of attacking mainland America: *Behind every blade of grass is an American with a rifle.* Some historians have disputed his exact quote or whether he even said such a thing at all. Myself, I believed it.

Having gotten no response from me, she just tapped my shoulder and pointed down to the trickle of blood coming over my shoe from the wound in my left leg.

"Yeah, I'm heading in." I started rolling my chair toward the door. "Gather up those weapons and take them into the magazine room."

"Okay, Grandpa. You want me to check the bodies for any identification?"

"Don't bother. Nobody's got a name any more. Everything belongs to the people. Individuals died a couple of years ago."

She shrugged away my philosophical musing.

"And tell your sister to take the backhoe out to that spot in the west parcel and dig a trench."

"Six feet down?"

Of course. I nodded. "Then you get the loader rigged up and start hauling those bodies toward their new home."

Jessica surveyed the scene again. "With seven, and the way they're laid out, it'll take two trips. That front bucket can only hold so much."

I nodded. "No hurry, as long as you have them in the ground before nightfall. Don't forget to switch back to the blade afterwards and level it off."

"Okay," she said, with a final look at the seven bodies. "Sissy's going to complain, you know."

I nodded. "Your sister doesn't like digging the trenches, but it's easier and quicker than the part you're doing."

After turning to head inside, she paused. "Will we ever run out of bad guys?"

"Well, with no more law and order, there's nothing to prevent these roving gangs from swarming across the land and destroying everything in their path. Somewhat like rabid locusts."

My granddaughter's expression was unreadable but she looked far older than her sixteen years.

"Would you zip into the magazine room and bring me another mag, honey? This one's mostly used up." With the safety on, I pressed the release catch and it dropped into my lap. One cartridge remained.

Jessica scurried inside and returned with two loaded fifteen-round magazines.

Placing one in my lap, I tapped the heel of the other to be sure all the cartridge bases were flush against the back of the magazine. Then I inserted it and pressed with my palm until it latched.

"I'll tell Sissy you said to dig the trench, but you know she's going to grumble." Jessica turned to head back inside. "How many trenches is that now, Grandpa?"

On the weathered rail beside me, I counted the notches. "Looks like nine so far." Since the inauguration of America's first socialist president, there had been no regular schedule of this type incident, but on the average we got a fresh group of gun-pointing freelancers about every seven weeks.

END

About the Yamamoto quote:

THE REFERENCED "LETTER" is claimed to be in the extensive personal files of Gordon W. Prange, the personal historian for Gen. Douglas MacArthur. The Yamamoto quote in this letter is said to be, "*to invade the United States would prove most difficult because behind every blade of grass is an American with a rifle.*"

https://napavalleyregister.com/news/opinion/mailbag/standing-by-disputed-quote-on-guns/article_0ebd672c-739c-562c-bb3f-8bb4e7ac9218.html

The Caves of Lonesanne Blu

Charles A. Salter

LORD OONAIN CAREFULLY placed the silk pouch with this ahn's profits inside the folds of his grey tunic. He locked the chain which bound the heavy erken doors of his store shut and limped down the street. Above him, the last glowing embers of a fiery red sunset filled the sky.

Twenty ahns ago, when he was a young man, he'd fought in the Terrible War and sustained grievous wounds, among them a battle axe which had hacked his left foot nearly in two. He'd lost three toes, but the rest had healed into a gnarled stub. It pained him always, especially so on cool misty nights when the fog rolled in from the dark ocean surrounding Lonesanne Blu. Less so on a clear night such as this, with the air fresh and sweet, the gnips chirping their mating songs, and the bright Orb of Danse overhead beginning to cast its golden light throughout the great city.

He hobbled as fast as he could down Oonain Mainway— named after him for his heroic exploits during the War—for he was almost late for his appointment with Warlord Rathe, in order to apply this ahn's profits to his old debt.

The street lay mostly quiet, though a few farmers still sat in their oxcarts, rumbling slowly towards their farms after selling wares in the marketplace, bent and weary and longing for their beds. But he heard a sudden commotion not more than a hundred paces ahead of him, where a small cluster of peasants jeered at something. A bamboo cage, within which stood a pitiable creature struggling for its life.

As Oonain drew near, he spotted Mahkoomba standing outside the cage, muttering curses and whipping at the wretched creature's hands as she struggled with the bamboo bars, trying to prevent the peasants from loading it into the back of an oxcart.

In a loud voice of command, the one he'd learned as a leader of warriors when he'd saved Warlord Rathe's life, he said, "What is the meaning of this disturbance, Mahkoomba?"

The old witch dropped her braided oxhair whip to her side and darted towards Oonain with head bowed, stopping short the required seven paces and bowing low. "A thousand apologies, Lord Oonain, but this wench owes Lord Rathe money she will not pay."

Oonain looked up from the old crone towards the cage. Within appeared to be a young woman with long black hair, but she was covered in thick grey mud from head to toe. "Is she comely, Mahkoomba? I have need of a wife."

"Yes, my lord. When clean, she has bronze skin like that of a war lance, almond-shaped eyes the color of darkest night. She has a melodious voice that could charm the very stones of the street. But—"

"Yes, Mahkoomba?"

"She is under sentence of death for refusing to pay her debts. At Lord Rathe's command, she is to be buried in the great pit in the caves of Lonesanne Blu this very night."

"What if I pay her debt, Mahkoomba?" *Surely such a young woman, not more than 17 or 18 ahns old, cannot owe much. And I need a wife. None of the young royals of Warlord Rathe's Imperial Court will marry a war invalid... they consider it a bad omen for future children to be born blind or without sense or without true allegiance to the great ancestors. As the old proverb goes, "A damaged tree produces weak seed."*

"Lord, she owes five hundred ducbhans."

Five hundred! Ay yi yi! It will take another ten ahns already for me to pay back Lord Rathe's loan for my shop. This will add another twelve. I will never be free of debt, for none of my ancestors have lived past sixty ahns. Still, this may be my one chance to at least leave heirs before I am buried with my ancestors in the Caves of Lonesanne Blu.

Oonain limped nearer the cage and could see a creature who still stood proud and tall, though so covered in mud he could not tell how she looked. He turned back to the old witch, who had followed seven paces behind and stood with her head still bowed. "What is the meaning of all this mud?"

"Our master, Warlord Rathe, decreed that she be humiliated by being dragged by oxen through the mire pit at the Imperial Pottery Works."

He turned back to the wretch. "Child, how did you accumulate so much debt?"

Before the young one could speak, the old crone broke in. "She took on the debt of her parents, my lord, who owed for food received during those ahns when they could not pay, since the old man lost his arm in the Terrible War."

"Is this true, child?"

She spoke. "It is, my lord. But after the death of my parents, when the wet winds last came, I sold our farm and home and gave every last ducbahn of the proceeds to Mistress Mahkoomba."

At this the witch shrieked, darted to the cage, and began thrashing at the young girl with her knotted whip. "Liar! You lie, wench! You tell falsehoods before the great Lord Oonain and deserve death tonight for that alone. You held back the precious Blu-stone of great value, mined from the quarry at Lonesanne Blu. If you had but sold that, too, you could have paid all your debt in full."

"I lie not!" she alleged firmly. The girl turned to Oonain. "My lord, when taking on the debt, I swore to sell the family farm and pay every last ducbhan of the proceeds, and I did. But the gemstone was the one and only family heirloom my parents left me, and they made me promise to keep it. It has been in our family since the time of the first ancestors who sailed here from the faraway place."

Oonain turned to the wrinkled old woman. "Why did you not simply confiscate the gem in payment and let her go in peace?"

"It would be accursed if taken forcibly. It would bring sure doom, perhaps even awakening the terrible mountain of fire. Lord Rathe said that if she would rather die than surrender it, then he would accept that decision and bury them both together."

Oonain pondered this, then spoke to the young prisoner. "Child, if I agree to pay your debt and set you free, do you agree to marry me, to bear my children, to work beside me in my shop, to stay with me 'til I return to my ancestors, full of ahns and ready to depart this domain of my own free will?"

"Will you marry me before all men as the royals do, on the High Hill, according to the custom of our ancestors?"

"That I cannot promise. I will beseech Lord Rathe for his permission, but I fear he will not grant it if you have angered him in the business of this great jewel. It would embarrass him before the Imperial Court if you were allowed full rights to attend the Court as the royal wife of Lord Oonain. But since the Terrible War, he owes me a special grant of request, which I have not claimed in twenty ahns now; I think it certain he will spare your life to live with me as a consort-wife, with all rights excepting those pertaining to the Royal Court."

"Then you would be banished from the Imperial Court, as well?"

"I would if he so decides. But that may not happen. I go to Lord Rathe this very night to repay another portion of my old debt, and I will ask him. I have other news for him which is very good, and he may feel kindly disposed towards me. If he is in a merry mood through drinking much vessen, he may be merciful and grant us a full royal marriage. But I will not ask unless you agree here and now to become my wife, whether greater or lesser, for I will not be shamed before the Court by being granted only a consort-marriage by him and then be told no by you later. Do you agree?"

"I agree, my lord."

"It is settled, then. What is your name, my child?"

"Sareela."

He smiled. "That is my deceased mother's name. This is a very good sign, a great omen of success for our pairing and life together. Our children may thereby escape the curse of the war wounded."

He turned back to the crone. "I shall return within the hour. You will cease from any further punishment of this girl until then, for she is now my betrothed. Do you understand?"

Mahkoomba bowed low. "Aye, my lord."

The girl turned towards Oonain as he started to limp away and stated, "Thank you, my lord. I promise you will be pleased with me 'til such day as we both are buried with our ancestors in the tombs of Lonesanne Blu, both full of ahns and ready to depart this domain of pain and tears."

AT THE PALACE, the captain of the guard waved Lord Oonain through. He soon came upon Warlord Rathe in his throne room, not seated, but laughing and mingling freely with the royals of his court. In one hand he held a huge goblet made of the finest rivnen mined from the high hills, from which wide brim occasionally splashed the light golden liquid of vessen as he turned this way and that, warmly greeting the members of his court, all preparing for the great feast.

Oonain beheld his master's visage and hearkened back 20 ahns to the Battle of the High Hill which ended the Terrible War. Traitor Sessenen, with his lieutenants and fiercest warriors, ignored all foes to left and right and stormed the hill where stood Warlord Rathe, his bodyguard, war commanders, and signal men. As Sessenen pressed the attack, Rathe's loyalists fell like strahnen till only three remained at the summit. Distracted by the bloody butchery surrounding him, Rathe did not see Sessenen swing his mighty battleaxe of torrenen. At the last moment, Oonain, with each hand gripping a kirksword of tempered rivnen painted black with quidblud poison, leapt between the two, freely accepting the wound intended for Rathe, while severing Sessenen's tattoed head before collapsing at the feet of his master.

Rathe soon spied Oonain limping among the noisy throng. Dressed in a royal tunic and breeches of gnu-hide, with a rivnen crown sporting huge Blu-stones, Rathe's fiery eyes flashed and he motioned with his free hand. "Lord Oonain! My friends, here is a man brave and true, the one to whom I owe my very life from the Terrible War! My friends, greet Lord Oonain with the honor he is due!"

As one, all the lords and ladies of the Imperial court puffed out their cheeks with great breaths of air and patted them with their hands, making a contented sighing sound, all the louder because so many at once, and the chamber of polished erkwood echoed with the sound until delicious shivers shot up Oonain's spine.

Despite his limp, Oonain walked tall and steady toward his master.

Drawing him aside with his free arm around Oonain's shoulder, Rathe said merrily, "What news, Lord Oonain?"

"Great news, my lord. With twenty ahns of peace, thanks to my lord's great skill at governance, the city grows and the countryside becomes richer, and my shop prospers more each week. I again have profits the double of what I had only one ahn ago. These will go far towards repaying my debt to you." He reached within his tunic.

"Tut! Discuss that with my treasurer and give him your wealth. I rejoice that you prosper and hasten towards the end of your debt. Is there anything I can do for you, my friend? I understand you have an interest in a young wench."

"News travels fast in the city, my lord."

"Indeed, it travels faster among those fleet of foot than among those laboring under old war wounds. Does it still bother you, my friend, as much as at the beginning?"

"It means nothing, my lord, compared to the pleasure of being in your presence, both of us still alive and healthy twenty ahns past the Terrible War."

The man smiled and nodded. "What of this wench, then?"

"My lord, I ask permission to pay her debt in full and then take her as my wife."

"I grant you life for life, Lord Oonain. Her life for mine. I pardon her in full."

Oonain bowed low in gratitude.

Rathe continued, "You may take her at once as your consort-wife, and may you be blessed with many fine children, sons who are warriors great as their father and storekeepers prudent and true like their father, to maintain the nation's prosperity."

Oonain bowed a second time. "Thank you, my lord. You are a great leader, wise, kind, and merciful. May I make one further addendum to my request?"

At that, Rathe frowned. "No, my friend, you must not speak of making her part of the Imperial Court. Do not let those words pass your lips, for I must not be humiliated before my court in the matter of a debtor holding back valuables that could pay a debt. No, you must never speak of this again. Enjoy your consort-wife, live, and be happy."

Oonain bowed deeply yet a third time, signifying eternal gratitude. "As you wish, my lord. I thank you with all my heart for granting this request and pledge again my utmost loyalty to you until such time as I return to my ancestors in the Caves of Lonesanne Blu."

⟡

LORD OONAIN RETURNED to the bamboo cage and was pleased to see the young woman sitting on the street, free of the cage, and that Mahkoomba had brought a bucket of water and cleaned most of the mud from Sareela's face and hair. The young one did have an appealing visage, he thought. Her skin was young, fresh, and without blemish. She had the shape of one who could bear many healthy children.

"Thank you, Mahkoomba," Oonain said. "Lord Rathe has granted me permission to make her my consort-wife. Her debt is now my debt, and the Warlord will be fully repaid all, even if it takes me twenty ahns more."

"I know, my lord. Lord Rathe sent a messenger ahead of you to inform me. She is now yours. Take her as you wish."

"Arise, my child," he said to the girl. "Come to your new home, Sareela."

"Aye, my lord." She struggled to stand up, but staggered as one leg buckled under her and collapsed into his strong chest.

"You are injured, I see," he said, glowering at the crone.

He picked Sareela up with both arms and carried her as one carries a babe, slowly down Oonain Mainway. Though his maimed foot moved slowly, and though he was 40 ahns old, he retained the legs and chest and arms of a warrior and bore her weight with ease.

He carried her over the threshold of his home beside the shop, sat her in a chair near a large erkwood tub, and ordered his servant girl to wash her fully and dress her in clean clothes.

When she was properly clothed, he returned to pour oil on and bandage her scrapes from the slough-drag and reddened welts from the knotted whip. She whimpered none but did shrink back in silence as he tightened each bandage. "Sareela, why did you not sell the gemstone so as to be free of your debt and save your life?"

"My mother made me promise not to sell or release the heirloom stone until the proper time had come."

"What time is that?"

175

"My mother pledged me not to mention the time until it had arrived, my lord."

"You must not call me lord, Sareela. You are not a servant. I have made you a free-woman and my consort-wife. You are bound to me not by chains of servitude, but by freely given pledges to remain until such time as I return to my ancestors in the Great Caves."

"By what shall I call you, then?"

"You may call me by the name given me by my father. Bravlin."

"Thank you, Bravlin. I promise you will be pleased with me."

TEN DAYS PASSED and her wounds healed. In her melodious voice, Sareela hummed sweet and sometimes sad songs of the stars and the Orb of Danse as she went about her business helping in the store, dispensing heavy sacks of licneed and laspar from the huge open-topped barrels, polishing and displaying household items made of erkwood and rich bowls, cups, and vessels made of shining rivnen. She soon displayed a knack for divining what customers might want, pulling just the right items from the shelves, and gaily describing them in such glowing terms that customers could not help but dispense their ducbhans and walk out clutching their bright new purchases with smiles on their faces.

Yet ten days, and the store was prospering already more than ever before.

Bravlin Oonain *was* pleased with her, but he waited ten days more so that the sight of him and his maimed foot might become more familiar to her and no longer cause alarm.

Twenty days it had been, when he locked the store at night, escorted her to their home next door, and said, "It is time, Sareela, to make our firstborn."

She said nothing, but loosened her satren and let it fall to the floor.

In the light of the oil lamp, he could see for the first time her fully naked form standing beside the bed. She had a fulsome, womanly body made for child-bearing and nursing of many healthy progeny.

He felt the excitement and strength he first had as a young warrior 20 ahns ago. He dropped his tunic and stepped near, caressing her gently in his arms. Her long black hair cascaded around her bronze shoulders, and her breath flowed soft and sweet.

He could feel both their hearts beating. His strong as a warrior, like a great beating of a war drum. Hers fluttering fast but light, much like a tiny eubird flitting about the room.

Afterwards he lay still on his back, feeling taller, stronger, and freer than the windswept hills overlooking the bay. For the first time in many ahns, his foot did not hurt.

She nestled in the crook of his left arm and sighed.

He felt sure they had made a son.

IT WAS RATHER A daughter, born at the appointed time. But he was not disappointed, instead finding himself enchanted by the tiny girl with almond-shaped eyes the color of midnight, just like her mother's. Her cry when hungry was soft and musical, like the tone of her mother's voice. Even the way she kicked her tiny arms and legs and struggled as they tried to dress her made him fall in love with the world all over again. He had not felt so happy since before the Terrible War.

They called her Sareela in honor of both her mother and grandmother. As soon as she could walk and talk, she helped out in the store, picking up stray picbeans which fell from the weighing balance as Bravlin poured out and packaged goods for his customers, and as Sareela collected the payments and left each customer smiling and departing the store feeling they had gotten the best bargain of their lives.

When the store was occasionally idle, the little one played under the counter with her furry friend Daneela, the great catcher of vermin, or crawled behind the counter and tugged on the pantaloons of her father, and begged to be held and told a story of the ancient days before her birth.

The store did so well that Bravlin opened a second one at the far end of Oonain Mainway, over by the docks where the fishing boats returned each evening with piles of grint, eening, and roonay.

Roonay was considered a delicacy at the Imperial Court, so Bravlin invested in buying more fishing boats and hiring more free-men, to fulfill a standing order from Lord Rathe himself to keep the Court supplied. This brought in more ducbhans than Bravlin had ever seen before, and soon the three of them—husband, wife, and tiny daughter—could barely manage everything involved in their business enterprises.

One night after returning weary from a long day at the store, Bravlin said, "Sareela, it is time to make our second child."

Removing her satren, she smiled and asked, "Do you think it will be a son this time?"

He smiled back. "It matters not. If the girl is as lovely and enchanting as my two Sareelas, we can have a dozen more... but I think we will run out of names in due course should that happen."

Afterwards, lying in bed, warm and content, looking out the window at the tall birnbaums swaying in the island winds, he no longer felt tired, but felt he had the strength of ten.

THE AHNS PASSED, and they had two sons and two daughters, and opened four shops in all, one for each heir to manage in due course. Bravlin was prosperous beyond his wildest dreams and had long ago, at the age of 53 ahns, paid off his debt to Lord Rathe, including the second debt to free Sareela.

Now he was nearly 60 ahns old and knew he would soon return to his ancestors in the Caves of Lonesanne Blu. There was a pain deep in his right side which sometimes stabbed horribly if he twisted a certain way while lifting heavy loads of picbeans.

He consulted with the physician of the Imperial Court, who informed him it was concenterra and was not curable by any medicine known on the island and that he should prepare himself for his final journey beyond the far horizon. He did not say a word of this to Sareela, but she seemed to know.

When he paused while weighing grain to grip his side as a painbolt shot through him, she stopped and stared, a sad look in her dark eyes. When she reached over in bed to take hold of him at night, he usually couldn't move other than to place an arm around her. He no longer enjoyed eating fresh roonay, but confined his diet mostly to plain boiled licneed.

178

One day after work, he gathered his four children, each now as old or older than Sareela had been when first he met her. Bravlin kissed them on their foreheads and blessed them and appointed them their respective shops to manage. He charged them always to heed their mother, placing her in charge of overseeing all the family enterprises. With his wrinkled palms on top of each head in turn, from oldest to youngest, he made a half-bow before each and then said farewell.

He asked Sareela to take him to the Caves of Lonesanne Blu. Eyes wet with tears, she agreed, but first darted to their bedroom to retrieve something.

They left their home by oxcart. Bravlin looked back one last time to see his children standing in the doorway, eyes wet with tears.

It was a slow journey, and every time the cart rolled over a stone or into a hole he gasped in pain.

The road became rougher as it wound around the hills formed by molten rivnen many ahns ago, leaving wide open channels in the rock as it refroze. A criss-cross network of damp caves resulted, each filled with the remains of many generations of their ancestors.

The Caves of Lonesanne Blu.

At the Oonain branch of the Caves, Sareela laid a gnu-skin on the rocky floor and helped Bravlin lie on top. She sat seven paces away, an oil lamp on the ground beside her.

He rolled his head to the side. "Seven paces, Sareela? You are my wife, my one true love. Come nearer."

She scooted closer without standing upright.

He continued, "I cherish the day we met and I could redeem you, my wife. As you promised, you lived with me, worked beside me in the store, and bore my children. As you promised I would be, I am truly pleased with you and have been greatly blessed by you. You are my one true love."

"Then it is time," she said simply in her musical voice, which sent one final shiver up his spine.

"Yes, it is my time to return to our ancestors. I depart this domain of my own free will."

"That, but also time to be released from my vow to my mother."

"You mean concerning the precious gemstone?"

179

She pulled the Blu-stone from her scarlet satren and held it in her hand.

Bravlin marveled at how it sparkled in the light of the oil lamp, each facet shimmering with beauty. A stone of great value, a stone large as the largest on Lord Rathe's crown.

"My mother said I could not give it up until the right time, nor could I explain what the right time was until it had come."

"My death is the right time?"

"No, my love. The time would be when I knew in my deepest of hearts, without any doubt, that I was in the presence of my one true love."

She placed the stone in his right hand, and he grasped it firmly.

"Take this with you to our ancestors, my love," she whispered, "and tell them I kept my vow and gave the stone only to the right one and at the right time."

END

Acknowledgements

THE AUTHORS ARE extremely grateful to *Dingbat Publishing* for contracting our collection of short stories. We have more stories in the pipeline and are hopeful they will also find a home here in the future. We're very pleased with the thorough and perceptive editing of Gunnar Grey, who found (and corrected) all our remaining manuscript flaws... while making our stories *read* even better. Thanks also to Gunnar Grey for a cover that conveys the sense of our anthology.

About the Authors

J. L. Salter

WRITING HAS BEEN my driving interest since about fourth grade. I love creating believable characters and turning them loose with interesting and/or humorous situations. The result has been romantic comedy, screwball comedy, romantic suspense, time-travel, and other science fiction.

Though this is my first collection of short stories, I've worked with three royalty publishers in releasing fifteen novels and four novellas. Released by *Dingbat Publishing*: "Double Down Trouble," "Curing the Uncommon Man-Cold," "Scratching the Seven-Month Itch"... and a novella, "One Simple Favor".

I'm co-author of two non-fiction monographs (about librarianship) with a royalty publisher, a signed chapter in another book, and a signed article in a specialty encyclopedia. I've also published articles, book reviews, and over 120 poems; my writing has won nearly 40 awards, including several in national contests. As a newspaper photo-journalist, I published about 150 bylined newspaper articles, and some 100 bylined photos.

Before I worked nearly 30 years in the field of librarianship, I was a decorated veteran of the U.S. Air Force (including a remote tour of duty in the Arctic, at Thule AB in N.W. Greenland).

Married, I'm the parent of two and grandparent of six.

Charles A. Salter

CHARLES A. SALTER HAS been a writer all his life. A professional member of the American Society of Journalists and Authors, he has published about two dozen fiction and nonfiction books and hundreds of articles in scientific journals, popular magazines, and newspapers, as well as numerous U.S. Government Technical Reports. His adult mystery novels and juvenile nonfiction books have earned excellent reviews and won various awards.

Currently retired, he served for 28 years as a Medical Service Corps officer in the United States Army. Following that, he spent many years as a civilian working at the military's medical school, the Uniformed Services University of the Health Sciences, where he helped manage major biomedical research programs.

He has often collaborated on writing projects with his brother J. L. Salter, and this is their third co-authored book. Living currently in Maryland, he is married, has three children and six grandchildren.

Also by J.L. Salter

Screwball Romantic Comedy
Not Easy Being Android
Stuck on Cloud Eight
Rescued By That New Guy in Town
Scratching the Seven-Month Itch
Curing the Uncommon Man-Cold

Screwball Comedy
Called to Arms Again
Size Matters

Time-Travel Romance
Cowboy Out of Time

Paranormal Romance
The Ghostess and Mister Muir

Romantic Suspense
One Simple Favor
Double Down Trouble
The Overnighter's Secrets

Holiday Romance
Random Sacks of Kindness

Contemporary Romance
Hid Wounded Reb
The Duchess of Earl
Pleased to Meet Me

War Fiction
Echo Taps

Also by Charles A. Salter

The Kare Kids Adventures
The Secret of Bald Rock Island
Charlotte and the Mysterious Vanishing Place
How Three Brothers Saved the Navy
The Travel Twins and the Lost Secret of the Vikings

The eBay Detective
The eBay Plot
The eBay Code
The eBay Guardian

Brad Stout Adventures
Borrowed Bones

Thanks for reading! Dingbat Publishing strives to bring you quality entertainment that doesn't take itself too seriously. I mean honestly, with a name like that, our books have to be good or we're going to be laughed at. Or maybe both.

If you enjoyed this book, the best thing you can do is buy a million more copies and give them to all your friends... erm, leave a review on the readers' website of your preference. All authors love feedback and we take reviews from readers like you seriously.

Oh, and c'mon over to our website:
www.DingbatPublishing.ninja

Who knows what other books you'll find there?

Cheers,

Gunnar Grey,
publisher, author, and Chief Dingbat

δ

Made in the USA
Middletown, DE
25 January 2020